Carl's Quest

PAGE PUBLISHING, INC.
Conneaut Lake, PA

First originally published by Page Publishing 2020

ISBN 978-1-64544-161-8 (pbk)
ISBN 978-1-64544-162-5 (digital)

Printed in the United States of America

Carl's Quest

LINDA BALLARD

Illustrations by
JASON BALLARD

CHAPTER 1

Long, long ago and far, far away, in a little forest nestled between a winding brook and the snowcapped mountains lived a young man by the name of Carl. He was hardworking, happy, and loved his forest and all the creatures living there.

Carl's home was a tiny wooden cottage that had one window and dirt floors. It was filled with handmade furniture lovingly carved by Carl. A round table surrounded with four chairs stood in front of an enormous stone fireplace that took up most of one wall. A bed stood in the corner of the wall opposite the door. Two very comfortable-looking chairs with arms sat in another corner with a table and lamp between them. Five well-used books lay stacked on the table. On the wall abutting the fireplace, a large chest of drawers stood next to a closet. There was a large basin atop one of the tables against this wall where Carl would wash his dishes. The fourth wall had the only window in the small cabin and boasted an ornately carved highboy and cabinets where Carl stored all his dinnerware and food supplies. He made each piece of furniture himself with wood he collected from trees that had fallen in the woods over the years. Carl would never cut down a tree as he loved them and the beautiful leaves they proudly wore. The trees also provided homes for his animal friends. Carl gathered the wood from fallen trees and neatly stacked it behind his cottage. When he had enough wood to carve a table or chair, Carl would take great care and build another piece to sell to the local villagers. They all admired his furniture as he would carve images of his animal friends who lived in the forest on each one. In fact, the animals were proud to pose for his carvings. They would chatter away with Carl while he painstakingly duplicated their features on each piece.

Every morning, Carl would rise before the sun came up, waking his little friends who lived in the beautiful trees and nested under the lush green bushes. He began each morning preparing fried eggs, crisp bacon, and buttered his home-baked bread in his cozy little kitchen area. He then put a small bowl of milk down on the freshly swept floor for his cat, Tommy, who enjoyed catnapping on the only little rug in the cottage that was to the right of the fireplace. Tommy rose slowly, stretched his legs, and lazily strolled to his bowl. He lapped up his milk and then sauntered over to where Carl was washing up the dishes after his breakfast. Tommy loved to rub against Carl's legs, just long enough until Carl had to wipe his hands on the towel and bend over to stroke Tommy's head and back. Satisfied, Tommy ran to the door, waiting impatiently for Carl to open the door and let the daily adventure begin.

"Have fun, Tommy, and don't get into trouble," warned Carl as he closed the door behind the cat.

Tommy ran out and into the woods. He too loved the woods and all the little creatures living there. Within minutes, Tommy saw his chipmunk friends, Sally and Arnold, who waited patiently for Tommy, and the three of them scampered away playing hide-and-seek. This was the daily routine for Carl and Tommy, and today was no exception.

After letting Tommy run off to play in the woods, Carl grabbed his old jeans jacket that was full of patches. He loved his old jacket and wore it almost every day. Each time Carl snagged his jacket on a broken branch of a tree, or ripped it while helping one of his little friends like Sammy the Skunk out of a tangle of bushes, Carl would sew it as soon as he could. Each patch was a reminder of his happy life and his wonderful friends.

Usually in the mornings, Carl gathered mushrooms, berries, fruits, and nuts from the trees and bushes in the forest and placed them neatly in softly curved light brown willow baskets getting them ready to sell to the villagers living nearby, but today was promising to be such a glorious day that he walked through the woods to the stream instead. The air smelled wonderful, the aroma of the sweet flowers all around. The sun had begun to peek through the trees. The sky was as blue as the sea, and there wasn't a cloud in sight. The yellow rays of the sun were already playing on the stream and making it glimmer and shine, reflecting the trees and bushes on both banks. The birds were already awake and flying around seeking berries and insects to feed their young. They were singing sweet songs to each other as they soared through the air. Carl looked longingly over the stream toward the majestic mountains in the distance. Between the bubbling stream and the tall, white-capped mountains, at the edge of the forest lay a tall, dark-green hedge filled with thorns and vines. Carl slowly walked toward the hedge.

The hedge was almost twenty feet tall and very thick. It went on forever in both directions. Carl had always been drawn to the hedge, longing to see what lies on the other side. He had heard wonderful stories about beautiful white swans with their long graceful necks gliding on a lake of shimmering silver with an enchanted castle just beyond. It had been said by the villagers that even though no one had been on the other side of the hedge for over one hundred years, that the stone castle was glorious with its tall turrets. It even had a drawbridge that arced over the lake and was the only entry to the castle. Others said that there were no swans or lake but only ugly, evil creatures that enjoyed inflicting pain on all who ventured their way. They were described as being short with huge shoulders, elongated arms, and long, extremely sharp teeth.

Ever since Carl could remember, he had had dreams about a beautiful maiden with long, blond tresses and a glorious smile that would melt the heart of the grouchiest grouch. He envisioned himself in fine clothes walking on the bridge across the shimmering silver lake as graceful, regal swans floated by. Carl imagined the bridge to be made of wide weathered oak planks and without any railings on the sides. The bridge ended at the foot of two huge gates made of pure gold that glistened in the sunlight. The gates slowly opened to greet him as he walked on the planks of wood crossing the lake. Then the beautiful maiden greeted him with a wondrous smile and a heart full of love. They embraced, and Carl had never been happier in his life. Then he woke up in his bed and realized it was just a dream.

Today, though, Carl felt like his dreams would come true. He must find a way to get over the hedges and seek the beautiful girl of his dreams. Carl had walked to the hedges many, many times, and he had noted that they were filled with long, thick, sharp thorns. The hedges were dense with vines intertwining the thorns. Carl walked back and forth in front of the hedges for quite a long time, thinking of how he could get to the other side. He finally sat down on a huge rock by the stream to look at the hedge and plan his climb.

The blue birds and robins had finished feeding their young and were flying around singing when they noticed Carl sitting there, looking so sad. Knowingly, they gathered around and flew above Carl in circles. Instead of singing, they started calling to each other, as well as to the sparrows, blue jays, and cardinals in the woods. Carl looked up surprised to see so many of his feathered friends circling overhead. They called to each other and to Carl. Then he noticed they were trying to show him something. They were laying out the way for Carl to scale the hedge. A blue jay flew down to a vine about a foot from the ground. Then a sparrow flew to another vine a little higher. A cardinal and then another sparrow each landed further up. They continued this until a robin landed on top of the hedge and called out loudly. Carl realized that they were pointing out the way for him to get over the hedge.

He stood up and walked to the hedges. Carl thanked them all and started to climb the hedge, carefully putting his right foot on the vine where the blue jay was perched. Then as soon as the sparrow flew off, he put his left foot on that vine. Carl continued up putting his foot on the vine where each bird perched and then flew off until he was just about a foot from the top of the hedge. He almost missed the spot where the wren had been sitting. This slip made the birds circle in close to Carl and call harshly to him. He realized his mistake, especially after a thorn ripped his jacket and almost scraped his skin. Carl was more careful after that.

When Carl reached the top of the hedge, he closed his eyes tight and hoped that when he opened them, he would see an enchanted castle and not any evil creatures. Carl slowly opened his eyes. The sun blinded him. Then as he blinked his eyes and shielded them with his left hand held over his brows, he caught a glimpse of a beautiful silver lake shimmering in the sunlight with not only a dozen white swans gliding across the water but two sleek black swans as well. The castle was enormous and had at least twenty turrets reaching to the skies. It was made of dark gray stone and had red and yellow and blue pennants flying from the highest point of each turret.

Between the hedge and the lake was a large expanse of lush green lawn. It looked like green velvet. There were little yellow and white daisies surrounding the lake. Carl had to hold his breath for a minute. He couldn't believe that the castle of his dreams lay before him. He closed his eyes twice and then opened them quickly, but the sparkling lake, graceful swans, and imposing castle did not disappear.

Tommy, becoming bored playing with Arnold and Sally had run up to the hedges. He looked up at Carl and meowed loudly. Tommy's meowing woke Carl from his entrancement at the wonder of what lay before him. He almost lost his hold and could easily have fallen. Realizing that it was getting late, and he could not continue over the hedge right now, Carl slowly climbed down the hedge. His friends, the birds, again showed him which vines to place his feet upon. With their help, it was a slow but safe climb for Carl back down the hedge.

As soon as Carl had both his boots firmly on the ground again, he scooped Tommy up and ruffled his soft fur. "You're right, Tommy," he said, stroking the cat. "It's time for your dinner. I will have to get prepared to continue on to the castle. Early tomorrow morning will be soon enough for my journey."

Carl walked happily through the woods to his small cottage, whistling all the way. Tommy walked beside Carl swishing his tail to say hello to all his forest friends. Carl smiled at Sammy Skunk, stopped to talk to Jill and Bill Deer and their son, Ricky, and pulled Chester out of a hollow in an old log. Chester was an old turtle—very, very old. No one knows how old Chester really is, but they all agree he is the oldest resident in the woods. Chester could not see well at all, and while he was sure-footed entering the log, when he tried to turn around, he got stuck. Chester was lucky Carl was passing the old log on his way back to the cottage.

As soon as Carl returned to the cottage, he laid a fire in the huge stone fireplace and set about starting his dinner. While his stew was simmering in the pot over the flames, he began sewing another patch on his jean's jacket that he snagged on the hedge thorns this morning. *"I can't wear my jacket with any rips in it when I enter the castle,"* he mused. *"I must polish my boots tonight,"* he added.

After dinner, Carl washed the dishes, shined his boots so carefully that his face shown back at him, and then went right to bed. Tommy fell asleep at the foot of the fire on his small rug. They both were contented after a full day. Carl dreamed again of the magical land over the hedge with the huge sparkling pond and the wondrous castle. He also dreamed that he was greeted by the beautiful maiden with golden hair and the warmest smile he had ever seen.

CHAPTER 2

Carl awoke very early in the morning with a song in his heart. He looked forward to his wonderful adventure. His whistling and bustling about in the kitchen was contagious. Tommy, too, was happy this morning, and he purred loudly when Carl bent down to rub his head. Last night, Tommy had dreamed he was dining on fish, freshly caught from the brook.

Today Carl changed his morning routine. After breakfast, he set about gathering tools and food to take with him on his adventure. Tommy's good mood slowly vanished. He was annoyed that Carl did not immediately open the kitchen door after breakfast. Tommy started switching his tail back and forth in little jerks and stood still in the middle of the cottage glaring at Carl. He gave an annoyed little "meow," but Carl didn't even seem to notice. Finally, Tommy ran over to Carl and reached up with his claws on Carl's leg and looked straight up into Carl's face as if to say, *"It is time to go outside."*

"Sorry, Tommy," said Carl. "I guess I forgot to let you out to play with your friends after breakfast."

As soon as Carl opened the door, Tommy shot outside and ran into the forest to play with Raymond Raccoon, Betsy Badger, and Sammy Skunk. They liked to play "catch me if you can." They all enjoyed it for most of the morning, but usually, Sammy Skunk would get so excited that he would forget he was playing with his friends and accidentally let his skunk perfume loose. Then they would all have to take a swim in the stream to get rid of the aroma. Still, since they had so much fun playing the game, they didn't really mind having to take a swim before lunch. It was much better than when Peter Porcupine played with them. Even though he never wanted to hurt anyone, Peter's little spikes hurt when they brushed up against him while running. They couldn't play "catch me if you can" or "tag, you're it" with Peter. When they played with Peter, it was usually "hide-and-seek," and Peter was the one elected to do the finding. It hurt them much less that way.

Carl took special care this morning while brushing his teeth. He looked into his small mirror as he was shaving to make sure he looked his best. The mirror reflected a good-looking young man in his midtwenties with a full head of brown hair with reddish highlights, serious blue-gray eyes, and a strong chin. He carefully combed his hair, making sure the part was straight and even.

Satisfied with his reflection, Carl then searched high and low in the cottage for his mother's gold locket. It was special to him, and he wanted to bring it as a present for the beautiful maiden. He searched all over the kitchen—in the sugar bowl, the flour canister, and the bread box. He looked on the mantle over the fireplace, on the table beside his favorite chair, in his dresser drawers. Carl was feeling sad because he could not find it. Then he remembered that he put it in a box, wrapped in paper, on the shelf in his closet. He dragged the chair from the kitchen area to the closet, climbed up on the seat, and put his hand on the shelf in the closet. He had to move several small boxes aside. Finally, he found the box he sought. Relieved, Carl retrieved the small gold locket and put it in the pocket of his jacket, gathered his bag with his lunch and tools, and happily went out the cottage door.

All the animals in the forest knew that Carl was going to return to the hedge beyond the stream this morning. They waved at him as he passed. Those that didn't wave followed along behind or ran on ahead. Carl was happy—happier than he had been in a long time. The huge pine trees were filled with birds and squirrels. Chipmunks and groundhogs waved from under bushes. Opossums hung upside down on branches and waved and called out good wishes. Turtles walked slowly behind while deer kept pace with him alongside the trail. Carl was almost walking on air, and he was smiling widely. By the time Carl reached the hedges, everyone was there and ready to help.

Carl sat down on the rocks by the stream to talk with his forest friends. He opened his pack and shared his lunch with them. He told them what he had seen the day before—the lawn of green velvet, the shimmering silver lake surrounded with pretty flowers, the elegant white swans, and the black swans, too, and of the majestic stone castle with the golden doors at the end of the wooden bridge. Carl happily said, "The villagers were right. There is an enchanted kingdom on the other side of the hedges and not ugly short evil creatures with huge shoulders, long arms, and long sharp teeth."

When they finished eating, Carl put the bag that held his tools over his shoulder and again climbed the thorny hedges with the help of his feathered friends following the birds' trail as he had the day before. When he reached the top, again he let out a huge gasp at how beautiful the scene was that lay before him.

Carl was very surprised to see that there were absolutely no sharp thorns on the other side of the hedge. That would make his descent so much easier than the ascent up the hedge. As he slowly disappeared from view climbing down the back of the hedge, all the animals wished him luck. The birds sang sweetly and flew in joyous circles through the leaves of the tallest oak trees.

CHAPTER 3

When Carl landed on the velvety green lawn, he could not believe how soft it was under his feet. He strode across the grass toward the castle smiling happily as he watched the swans gliding smoothly on the silver lake leaving trails of soft ripples reflecting the sun behind them. Beautiful flowers of yellow, red, pink, and white surrounded the lake. He was mesmerized by the beauty of his surroundings. Carl counted eight of the twenty turrets bearing colorful pennants. When he approached the shimmering lake, several of the swans gracefully swam close to the shore as if to say, *"Hello and welcome."* Carl stood by the sweetly smelling flowers, his newly shined boots reflecting their glorious colors, and watched the elegant swans swimming across the lake for several minutes.

Then he walked to the planked bridge leading to the castle gates. He took a deep breath and purposely put his left foot on the wooden planks. It made a deep solid sound. It was all he could do not to run across the bridge. Carl walked briskly across the planks to the foot of the golden gates, his boots sounding a steady thump, thump, thump with each step he took. He stopped at the golden gates looking from bottom to top in awe of the intricate designs laid thereon. And as his gaze lifted from the base of the gates to the top, they slowly began to open for him to enter.

The huge doors opened wide. The interior of the castle lay beyond. But there was no beautiful maiden with golden hair and warm smile waiting to greet him. Carl had dreamed of this moment for such a long time. He couldn't believe that she was not there. He closed his eyes tight and held them closed for several seconds. Then he opened them. But she still was not there. Carl did the only thing he could do. He passed through the doors and strode into the castle.

Carl found himself in a well-manicured courtyard. There were flowing fountains and sculptures dispersed throughout the formal flower beds filled with an array of colors. Perfectly carved topiaries of hedge bushes in the shapes of fanciful animals were in the center of each corner flower bed. He saw a unicorn in the middle of the bed on the left. There was a horse with wings in the center of the bed on the right. In the far left corner was a dragon, which looked like it had flames coming right out from the dragon's mouth. A fairy with delicate wings was sculpted in the middle of the far right flower bed. Each flower bed was filled with red tulips, white lily of the valleys, blue bells, yellow marigolds, and pink pansies.

Beautiful music seemed to float all around Carl. He couldn't tell which direction it came from at first. Then he noticed off to his right between the winged horse and fairy topiary flower beds that people were gathered together on the other side of an archway leading to a great hall. Everyone wore gaily colored clothing, and they were moving to the music. Some were dancing. Some were just laughing. A few were talking happily among themselves. As Carl slowly approached the group, they turned toward him and parted, backing away, leaving a pathway for him to move through them. At first Carl was worried as he was a stranger, but they had smiles and nods of greetings for him. In the center of the gathering was the beautiful golden-haired maiden of his dreams.

Carl could only smile and stare at the lovely vision in front of him. She was tall and thin, with eyes the color of the deep blue sea, long golden curls, and the biggest, warmest smile he had ever seen. This beautiful maiden was wearing a dress that matched the color of her exquisite eyes. She was so special that Carl imagined she must be a princess. She motioned for Carl to come forward and held her delicate hands out to him. As Carl walked toward her she moved toward him, as if floating on a cloud. Carl's heart almost stopped beating he was so happy. His dream had come true.

While looking deeply into her sparkling blue eyes, and just as the tips of their fingers touched, Carl felt a hand grasp his shoulder. He immediately whipped his head to the right to see who had interrupted the most perfect moment of his life. He gazed directly into the eyes of a formidable-looking man with wavy white hair topped with a large jewel-encrusted crown. Over his shoulders, he wore a long red velvet cape edged in white ermine. It immediately registered to Carl that this must be the king of this castle. Carl bowed his head and dropped to his left knee and stammered, "Y-y-your Majesty."

"Please rise," ordered the king in a deep even voice.

For a few moments, both Carl and the king quietly observed each other. The music had stopped, and there was a hush over the great hall. No one spoke. No one moved. It seemed that no one breathed. Time almost stood still.

Carl did not notice at first, as he only had eyes for the beautiful princess in the blue gown, but he now realized that he was surrounded by the king's royal guards. They were all dressed in military clothing of royal blue with white trim. Each guard wore a long sword sheathed in a scabbard attached to a white belt around his waist. Every one of them had their right white-gloved hand crossed in front of them holding onto the hilt of the sheathed sword, ready to pull the sword out at a second's notice. Forty eyes stared directly at Carl, not one blinking, awaiting orders from the king. All the revelers had already backed away from Carl and were gathered in little groups on the outside of the royal guards' newly made circle around Carl and the king. It stayed so quiet that Carl felt he must be deaf. Not a sound could be heard.

Carl stole a look around but could not see the beautiful princess anywhere. Then out of the corner of his right eye he caught a movement of blue. Stealing a quick glance in that direction, he saw the princess being escorted by two royal guards hurriedly through a large wooden plank door. Then she had disappeared from sight.

CHAPTER 4

"Are you friend or foe?" inquired the king in a steady deep voice, while looking fiercely into Carl's eyes.

"I am most definitely a friend, Your Majesty," said Carl evenly.

At a signal from the king, his royal guards backed up a few paces, still keeping their eyes glued on Carl and their hands on their sword hilts. The group of people slowly moved closer to Carl and the king. They seemed to relax a little upon hearing that Carl came as a friend.

"I am King Stephen, ruler of the realm of Alauria. From what land do you come from and for what purpose have you entered my kingdom?" inquired the king, tilting his head ever so slightly and looking deeper into Carl's eyes.

Carl did not want to tell King Stephen that he was here to find the beautiful maiden of his dreams, who was quite possibly the king's daughter. On the other hand, he did not wish to lie to the ruler of his wondrous land.

"I come from the woods on the other side of the great hedges," said Carl. "I have no purpose other than to admire your wonderful kingdom," he added. This was completely true as Carl thought this astonishing new world he found himself in was the finest kingdom imaginable.

Clearly, King Stephen was relieved with Carl's answers and believed all that Carl had proclaimed. He signaled to his royal guards to return to where they were before Carl arrived. The men, women, and children started to talk among themselves again in muted voices.

Music began to play again. Carl looked to his right and saw that the small group of musicians was about fifty feet away and between a set of closed double doors and the large wooden plank door through which the beautiful maiden had disappeared several minutes ago. The musicians were clad in dark blue uniforms with brass buttons on the sleeves, across their chests in an X shape and also on their shoulders. Carl had never heard such wonderful music as the royal musicians played or ever seen so many fine instruments. It was a magical touch to his first encounter in this new and delightful kingdom. The villagers near Carl's woods played crude wooden instruments and sang folksy ballads. They did not have such finery in their dress or melodies.

"Come dine with me and my daughters, Charlotte and Audrey. We shall talk of your kingdom as we entertain you. We have so few guests from afar," said the king kindly. "But first, as you must be tired from your journey, please accompany Lord Lawrence to the preparation rooms," said King Stephen to Carl as he nodded his request to a tall handsome man clad in elegant finery who was about the same age as Carl, standing a few feet to the king's left.

"Thank you, most kindly, sire," said Carl with a slight bow to King Stephen. Carl then turned to follow Lord Lawrence. As Carl walked off to the left behind Lord Lawrence, he glanced back to the door where the beautiful maiden had disappeared, hoping for another glimpse of her, but to no avail.

Lord Lawrence strode off with huge steps allowing for his tall stately manner and led Carl down a long stone walled corridor, past many doors on both sides. There were swords and shields with a single rose and swan emblazoned on each hanging between the doors. As they approached the fifth door on the right, Lord Lawrence stopped, opened the door, and indicated that Carl should precede him inside.

"My servants will see that you are properly cared for. I shall return to accompany you to the dining hall in one hour. As you are aware, I am Lord Lawrence," he said with a questioning look toward Carl.

Carl realized that he had not properly introduced himself to Lord Lawrence, or the king, either, for that matter. "Please accept my apologies for not introducing myself to you sooner. I am Carl from the woods on the other side of the great hedges, and I am very happy to be in Alauria," smiled Carl.

Lord Lawrence looked at Carl and said kindly, "In one hour then." He turned and promptly left the room.

As Carl stood just inside the doorway, several people began to hurry toward him. One clearly wanted Carl to take off his boots while another was removing Carl's jacket from his back. Two men brought in large pails of water with steam floating off the top. They poured the hot water into a large wooden tub that was situated in the middle of an enormous room. After they removed Carl's clothing, they helped Carl climb into the tub. This was an unusual treat for Carl as he was used to bathing in the cool waters of his brook. When he finished washing, he was brought a huge towel with which to dry himself. Clean clothing was laid out on a large settee for him. Carl had never seen such finery. His own boots had a shine on them every day but not like the ones waiting for Carl to put on. These shone like glass. The shirt was crisp and white, the jacket and pants both deep green in color, soft in texture, and exquisitely tailored.

There was a knock on the door, and when one of the servants opened it, Lord Lawrence looked Carl up and down, smiled, and said, "You look like one of the royalty. The clothes I selected fit you perfectly."

At that moment, a loud gonging noise rang out. It sounded like it came from far down the hallway. "We must hurry or we will be late for dinner," said Lord Lawrence.

He led Carl back toward the great hall where the murmur of many voices grew louder and louder as they approached the hall. But upon reaching the great hall, no one was in sight. Carl noticed a huge gong to the left of the double doors that were now opened wide. Carl looked through the doorway and could see that people were dressed in fine clothing and talking animatedly and happily inside another enormous room.

When Carl and Lord Lawrence walked through the double doors, he was amazed at what he saw. On one side of what was apparently the dining hall, the royal musicians dressed in their finery were playing delightful music. On the other side of the hall was a huge wooden table, about thirty feet long, covered with more food than Carl had seen in his entire life. There was a gold goblet and white porcelain plate in front of each chair. King Stephen was seated in the middle of the far side of the largest table. On his right sat a beautiful girl with luxurious, long, dark brown hair. She was a vision in a red gown. Her eyes were emerald green and she had the most delightful smile. There were three empty seats on the left side of the king. All of the other chairs, probably forty at least, were filled with gaily talking men and women in beautiful finery.

On each side of the massive wooden table were two smaller tables with men, women, and children, happily chatting, laughing, and drinking from silver goblets. Many of those seated at these tables were the royal guards that Carl saw this afternoon.

There were ten royal guards standing at full attention, five on each side of the double doors. The floor in the center of the room had the single rose and swan design carved in wood. This was the same insignia Carl had seen on the shields hanging in the hallway. The rose and swan apparently was the crest of this wondrous Kingdom of Alauria.

Carl looked all around the enormous room, three times, and was disappointed that his beautiful vision in blue was not anywhere in the dining hall.

CHAPTER 5

Lord Lawrence brought Carl to where King Stephen was seated and whispered in the king's ear. The king nodded and turned to Carl. "Please be seated here on my left. I see Lord Lawrence has taken good care of you. You look splendid," said King Stephen graciously to Carl.

"Thank you, Your Majesty," replied Carl with a slight bow before he sat down.

Lord Lawrence sat on Carl's left, leaving the chair on the other side of him empty.

The gong sounded again. A hush fell over the great dining hall. King Stephen stood up and said loud enough for all to hear, "Tonight we have a special guest joining us. Everyone, raise your goblets and welcome Carl from the kingdom in the woods on the other side of the great hedge."

Many voices spoke out "welcome" as all faces turned toward Carl, and every man, woman, and child in the dining hall lifted their goblets. Carl raised his goblet in return, smiled broadly at them, and then drank. It was the sweetest apple juice he ever tasted. Carl thought that it must have a little honey mixed in it. As soon as he emptied his goblet of the delicious juice, it was immediately refilled by one of the servers.

Platters of food were passed around, and everyone filled their plates with lots of fruits, assorted vegetables, fish, and meats. As Carl ate the food, he found that each mouthful was tastier than the one before. The food was absolutely delicious.

Carl noticed that periodically almost everyone in the room would steal a glance over at the empty seat next to Lord Lawrence and would lose the smile on their faces. The king ate hurriedly and rose quickly after finishing his food. He did not speak to anyone during the dinner and looked displeased. Carl didn't think that he did anything wrong, and he wanted to know what was bothering King Stephen.

Leaning close to Carl, the king said, "I have affairs of state to attend to." He went on to say, "I must take leave immediately."

King Stephen stood and said, "Lord Lawrence will show you to your quarters after dinner." He then turned and left the table, hurriedly crossing the room and quickly leaving through the double doors.

After King Stephen left the dining hall, some of the children got up from their tables and started to play tag and other games while their parents danced to the music played by the royal musicians. But a majority of the people gathered their children and quickly left the dining hall.

Lord Lawrence rose and walked over to the beautiful dark-haired girl in the red gown. He offered her his arm and brought her to where Carl was sitting. Carl immediately stood up and smiled at this lovely vision. "I have the honor of introducing her Royal Highness Princess Audrey, the youngest daughter of King Stephen," said Lord Lawrence.

"I am most honored to make your acquaintance, Your Royal Highness," said Carl as he bowed to the princess. "And I am very happy to be here in Alauria," he added.

"The princess and I are engaged to be married," Lord Lawrence said softly as he smiled at Princess Audrey who beamed back at him with a big smile. Her eyes seemed to be dancing with happiness.

Then as quickly as she showed her happiness, her eyes saddened, and she said to Carl, "Please forgive me for rushing off, but I have something important to attend to. Please remain and enjoy the food and dancing."

As Lord Lawrence was escorting Princess Audrey away, he called back over his shoulder to Carl, "I shall return shortly and show you to your quarters."

Carl continued to search through the remaining people gathered in the dining hall for a glimpse of the beautiful girl of his dreams, but she still had not appeared. Within five minutes Lord Lawrence returned and asked Carl, "What are you looking for so intently?"

"I must confess, Lord Lawrence, that I saw the most beautiful vision in the world, the maiden of my dreams, when I first came to Alauria. She disappeared shortly thereafter. I will never be happy again until I find her," said Carl. "She has long golden curls and eyes like the color of the deep blue sea. When she smiles it warms my heart," continued Carl.

"Let us leave the dining hall. I have many things to tell you when we are alone," said Lord Lawrence very somberly.

Lord Lawrence led Carl back through the great hall to the stone hallway they were in before. They strode past the room Carl bathed in and continued down the hallway past seven more doors. On the right was a large staircase leading up to a gallery with many more doors. They climbed the stairs, and Carl looked down from the gallery to what must be the royal library. A huge candle-lit chandelier glistened in the center of the room. There were books on all four walls from the floor to the ceiling with only one window and one door on each side. Carl found it hard to believe there were so many books. He only owned a handful of books that he read and reread on days when the weather was so harsh it was impossible to leave his cottage. In the middle of the large library were many benches and tables where one could sit and read. On each table was a candelabra filled with ten candles to provide adequate light for reading. Several large carpets were scattered throughout the room so as to muffle the noise of boots clicking on the stone floor and not disturb people while they were reading. Even though it was an enormous room, it was warm and inviting and seemed cozy.

They continued walking around the gallery, and then Lord Lawrence stopped in front of the fourth door on the left. "I trust this room will be to your liking," said Lord Lawrence to Carl.

The room was at least twice the size of Carl's cottage in the woods. There was a huge four-poster bed with a canopy on top against one wall. He walked over to the double windows opposite the door to gaze down at a courtyard below that was filled with flowers, benches, fountains, and statues of little woodland creatures. It was a magical scene. Turning back to the room, he saw Lord Lawrence had seated himself in one of the two overstuffed chairs in front of a vast fireplace that had a roaring fire blazing within. A wooden shield bearing the single rose and swan hung above the mantle.

"Please come and sit here with me so I may tell you of a serious matter concerning everyone in Alauria," instructed Lord Lawrence to Carl.

CHAPTER 6

"Princess Charlotte is missing. I imagine that she is the beautiful maiden you speak of. The princess is the eldest daughter of King Stephen. We fear that she has been kidnapped by Baron Nelson of Grimalka," explained Lord Lawrence. "Not only is Princess Charlotte beloved by all, as she is the eldest daughter of the king, when she weds her husband will become the future ruler of Alauria," continued Lord Lawrence.

He rose and began pacing around the room while telling Carl about the princess. "The citizens of Alauria fear that if Baron Nelson had kidnapped the princess, he will force her to become his bride. Then he will let nothing stand in his way to reign over Alauria, including killing King Stephen. Baron Nelson is an evil person."

Carl asked, "What can we do to rescue Princess Charlotte?"

Carl was so upset to learn the girl of his dreams was in danger and may be lost to him forever. He knew he was right in his feeling that this beautiful girl was indeed a princess. Carl immediately stood up and started to walk around the room quickly back and forth from the windows to the fireplace and back again. "We *must* save her *now!*" he demanded.

Lord Lawrence walked over to Carl, put his hand on Carl's shoulder, and asked Carl to accompany him to the king's quarters where he said, "The king and his royal guard are planning ways to rescue the princess."

As Lord Lawrence and Carl raced through the gallery, down the stairs, along the corridor and to the great hall, Lord Lawrence explained to Carl that the princess disappeared yesterday afternoon when Carl arrived. "Apparently, the baron took advantage of your unexpected arrival diverting attention from him to whisk Princess Charlotte away. Everyone has been very upset over her disappearance, and all have tried to keep up courage for the king's sake."

They crossed the great hall to a wide curving staircase that Carl realized must lead to the king's private quarters. The staircase was adorned on each side with portraits of King Stephen and Princess Charlotte and Princess Audrey as well as many other royal figures he did not know. At the top of the stairs, two royal guards stood on either side of a set of great doors each bearing a carving of a single rose and a swan. Seeing Lord Lawrence and Carl rushing up the stairs, one of the royal guards immediately knocked two times and opened the doors.

King Stephen was seated on a bench under a wall of windows. Standing in a group in front of him were at least thirty-five royal guards as well as several other people that Carl remembered seeing in the dining hall. The room was so large that it did not seem crowded even with so many people standing in it.

The four-poster bed with the canopy was triple the size of the one in Carl's room. A round oak table was in the center of the room surrounded by at least twenty sturdy carved chairs. There was an overstuffed couch covered in red velvet that could seat eight people facing the largest stone fireplace Carl had ever seen. A tall man could walk inside the fireplace and not have to stoop over. Again, the seal of the kingdom, a single rose and a swan, was hanging over the mantle. A wrought iron chandelier with a hundred lit candles hung from the center of the domed ceiling. Even though it was evening, the light the candles provided made it seem like a bright sunny day at noon time.

Through the double doors on one of the walls, Carl could see Princess Audrey lying down on a white satin chaise lounge in what appeared to be her bedchamber. She was being attended to by several well-dressed ladies-in-waiting. They all were hovering over the princess and seemed quite upset themselves.

King Stephen ordered the royal guards from his room. He told them to, "Report back anything no matter how trivial, immediately." He motioned to Lord Lawrence and Carl to come to him as the others were leaving his quarters. Two of the royal guards remained.

King Stephen told Carl, "These are two of my most trusted guards. We are discussing any and all tactics available to us. I am sorry that you came to us at such a troubled time. You must be missing your family and wish to return to the woods beyond the hedge soon. We shall escort you back to your home first thing tomorrow morning."

"Your Majesty, I am deeply troubled as the baron used my arrival in Alauria to kidnap your beautiful daughter," said Carl. "I will do anything, anything at all to bring her back safely to you. You have but to tell me what to do or where to go, and I will pledge my life to return Princess Charlotte to you."

As much as Carl really would miss little Tommy and all his woodland friends, he feared the loss of the girl of his dreams even more. Carl vowed he would not return to the woods until Princess Charlotte was returned to her father unharmed.

"And I, too, will do anything to rescue Princess Charlotte," said Lord Lawrence. "Princess Audrey and I will not wed until her sister is safely home again. I know that you have instructed me to stay by her side, to protect her, but I assure you that Princess Audrey feels the same as I. She wishes me to find Princess Charlotte and soon."

"In that case," said King Stephen, "I instruct you to advise Carl of all the dangers as well as the tactics available to us. You are to take two of my royal guards to assist you and Carl in your endeavors. If you need any more help, do not hesitate to ask. All will be granted."

Lord Lawrence and Carl immediately left the king's quarters and ran down the royal staircase and through the great hall, along the long hallway, up the stairway to the gallery, and into Carl's room. Shortly after they arrived, two of the king's royal guards appeared at the door, knocked, and requested permission to enter.

"Sir Paul is the king's finest swordsman," said Lord Lawrence indicating the tall, red-haired man standing in front of them. "Sir Rodney has won every jousting tournament he has entered on behalf of King Stephen and Alauria."

Sir Rodney was slightly shorter and stouter than Sir Paul, and he had jet black hair and a full black mustache. They both wore the military garb of royal blue with white trim and long swords sheathed in scabbards hanging from a white belt around their waists. They each even wore a royal blue hat trimmed with one long white plumed feather atop it. They stood tall and proud in front of Lord Lawrence and Carl.

"Come in quickly. We must now discuss our plans to rescue the fair Princess Charlotte," spoke Lord Lawrence sternly.

CHAPTER 7

The four of them talked and planned until dawn broke. Carl was stunned to hear all about the evil Baron Nelson of Grimalka. The baron was a vile person who had a powerful wizard as his advisor. In addition to the baron's personal army, the wizard had an army of ugly creatures who did his bidding with great glee. The more evil their actions, the happier they were.

Grimalka was the kingdom on the other side of the mountains behind Alauria. Trees and flowers did not flourish in Grimalka. Instead, Grimalka's countryside was filled with huge rocks and misshapen plants with few leaves and no flowers. It was dark, gloomy, and looked dead. Many of the creatures lived in underground caves and fed on mushroom-like growths. It had been rumored that Baron Nelson himself was one of the creatures and that Dreaddrick the wizard enchanted the baron to appear in a human form so he could move among the residents of Alauria with ease. Grimalka had a castle, high on the tallest mountaintop overlooking the Near-Dead Swamp that was filled with slithering creatures. It was supposed to be impossible to reach Grimalka alive without help from the wizard, Dreaddrick. The wizard was said to live in the Black Forest that lay between Alauria and Baron Nelson's castle.

As Lord Lawrence was familiar with the stories all about the baron and his environs, it was agreed that Lord Lawrence would be in charge of the group with Carl as his second in command. Carl brought his knowledge and experience of living in the woods to the group. All four of the men sent for clothing worn by the villagers who farmed the pastures surrounding Alauria so they could move unknown and with ease through any and all terrain and villages in their crusade to save Princess Charlotte. Along with the simple clothing, the king had various weapons and tools packed into knapsacks for the men to carry on their backs. Carl proudly was wearing his jean's jacket that bore the patches of many important events in his life thus far. He also was carrying the tool kit he brought with him from home.

In order to appear as villagers on their journey, Lord Lawrence was henceforth to be known as "Larry." Sir Paul and Sir Rodney were to be called only "Paul" and "Rodney." No one was to know they were emissaries of King Stephen on a quest to save Princess Charlotte. They did not want any word of their existence to reach the ears of Baron Nelson. It was better that the baron believe that only King Stephen's royal guard were searching for the princess. In that respect, the king had commissioned a group of his royal guard to begin a thorough search for the princess. They left Alauria the prior evening. They would begin by thoroughly searching every village and farmhouse in the kingdom.

In midmorning, King Stephen and a handful of his most loyal subjects walked outside the castle to the royal stables. Princess Audrey and her lady-in-waiting were already in the stable courtyard talking with Lord Lawrence. They were joined by Sir Rodney's wife, Lady Rosemary, and their two children, Sarah and Christopher. They all stood and watched as four of the king's best steeds were saddled and made ready with food and water in leather bags placed across their backs. The saddles were plain leather without any royal crests on them to help maintain anonymity for the men. The horses were then led to Carl, Larry, Paul, and Rodney who were in a hurry to start their venture.

"We shall not return until we have rescued Princess Charlotte," said Lord Lawrence with a full bow to King Stephen.

"We assure you that she shall not be harmed, sire," added Carl. "I give you my word." Carl then bowed to King Stephen and climbed onto his steed, quickly followed by Larry, Paul, and Rodney. Princess Audrey rushed over to Lord Lawrence. He bent down from his saddle, kissed her, and promised to return safely to her very soon.

The king and his subjects somberly watched their four valiant heroes ride off toward Grimalka and did not move until they were no longer in sight.

CHAPTER 8

Larry and Carl rode in front while Paul and Rodney were only a few feet behind them. They headed directly toward the mountains of Grimalka, not using any of the roads intertwining through various villages in Alauria. They decided to stay away from as many people as possible so that word would not get out about four strangers traveling toward Grimalka. They also tried to avoid any farmhouses along the way.

The weather was clear and dry and not too warm. In fact, it was perfect weather for riding, and thus it made their journey a little easier. On the other hand, the king's royal guard was to ride to all the villages and farmhouses in the kingdom in their quest for the princess. They would leave no stone unturned.

A little past nine o'clock in the evening, they decided to camp for the night and let their horses rest. After unsaddling the steeds, they brushed them down and fed and watered them before setting about to feed themselves. Without their trusty horses, they could not accomplish their mission, so the welfare of their horses was of primary importance.

While lying down under the stars, Carl could not sleep. His first thoughts were of Princess Charlotte and the difficult adventure ahead of them on her behalf. His thoughts also kept wandering back to Tommy, his cat, and all his woodland friends. Carl knew that while he was gone, Tommy would live in the woods with Sally and Arnold Chipmunk and their family. Mrs. Chipmunk was a good mother and watched over Sally and Arnold all the time to make sure they were safe and happy. If anything happened in the woods, all the animals would work together to protect each other. But Carl still missed every one very much. He even missed Sammy the Skunk who would sometimes emit his special perfume accidentally while playing with his friends, making everyone stop playing and run to the brook to wash off. Carl finally drifted off to sleep and happily dreamed visions of Princess Charlotte's beautiful blue eyes and warm smile.

CHAPTER 9

Before the sun rose, Paul and Rodney covered the last embers of the fire they lit the night before with dirt to insure that the woods would not catch fire after they left. They also did not want to leave an easy trail for anyone to follow in case Baron Nelson had any of his evil creatures wandering around. All four of the men had eaten a small breakfast and were in their saddles when the first rays of sunlight broke through the trees.

The men rode for four days through beautiful countryside and lush green forests. All the animals they met along their ride wished them great success and offered them warnings about terrible Baron Nelson and the evil wizard Dreaddrick.

On the fifth day after passing through a thick forest, they could see huge rocks and large trees without leaves in the far distance. The closer they rode toward this, the gloomier it all appeared. Carl had never seen anything like this, even after some of his own woods caught fire from a lightning storm when Carl was a young man. When the fire finally died out, there was nothing but blackened trees all around. The forest directly in front of them looked gloomier than that.

While riding through the woods these past few days, the men saw many deer, rabbits, raccoons, skunks, chipmunks, turtles, and a large variety of songbirds. There were beautiful woodland flowers and happy sounds of animals at play. But Carl was sure that Grimalka's Black Forest would not have any such happy creatures, only ones that he feared would be evil in nature.

Lord Lawrence, seeing the look on Carl's face as he was staring at the rocks ahead of them, said to Carl gravely, "We shall see things you never would have believed existed. I, myself, have not been here before, but many stories have been told and passed along over the years. None of them are happy."

As they approached the rocks, Carl could see that they were not simply rocks but huge boulders. They would have to climb over them very carefully to get to the dark woodland behind them. Since it was approaching nightfall, Lord Lawrence said, "Let's camp here for the night. We will get an early start in the morning."

So as not to be detected, they did not light any fire to warm them during the night, nor to cook their dinner. Instead they finished the dried bread in the bottom of their packs for supper, saving a few crumbs for their breakfast. Paul and Rodney fished out the last of the apples in their packs and fed them to the horses.

In the morning, Lord Lawrence announced, "Leave the horses unsaddled. Take what packs and weapons you think we may need and find ways to strap them onto you so that your arms will be left free for climbing and fighting. We go on foot from here on."

"But what about the horses?" asked Carl. "We can't just leave them here unattended. They need…"

"The royal guards have been instructed to come here and bring the horses back to Alauria," interrupted Rodney.

"The guards also will leave provisions for us for when we reemerge from the Black Forest," added Paul.

"This was all planned ahead by King Stephen's royal guards before we left on our quest," said Lord Lawrence. "And every day, one of the royal guards will come here to check if we have returned. He will then signal for fresh horses to be brought here within the next twelve hours for our return home to Alauria."

Much relieved after hearing these plans, Carl was more than ready to continue their search for Princess Charlotte, and the sooner the better.

Paul pulled out all the ropes they had in their packs and tied them together. He said, "I will go first and find something to anchor the lead rope to and come back." With that, Rodney boosted Paul up the smallest boulder they saw and handed the end of the rope to Paul as he leaned over from the top, lying on his stomach. Paul stood up and then disappeared from sight.

After half an hour, Paul suddenly reappeared, dangling the end of the rope over the boulder. "Grab on and climb up. The other end is anchored to a huge stump about thirty feet from here," called down Paul.

Larry was the first to climb after checking that all his packs, gear, and weapons were tightly adhered to him and would not be in his way while scaling the large rock. As soon as he reached the top of the rock, Rodney motioned for Carl to climb next. Since Carl was an expert outdoorsman living his entire life in the woods, he easily climbed the boulder. Rodney pulled up the end of the rope after he arrived at the top.

When the four had finally gotten over the first ridge of boulders, they could see the stump Paul had anchored the rope around. It was about six feet high and almost four feet in width and was black as night. In fact, the Black Forest seemed to begin at this precise location.

Paul removed the rope, and Rodney untied the sections of rope. He handed a large segment of rope to each of the men and said, "Stow this portion of rope in your pack in case you need it later on." He added, "We do not know what looms ahead and what resources will be necessary."

As the four men walked only five feet into the Black Forest, sunlight disappeared even though it was high noon and the sun was shining brightly. It was dark as night inside the Black Forest. In fact, where the few clouds in the sky over Alauria were white and fluffy, the clouds over the Black Forest were thick, black, and ominous looking.

Larry took two very hard rocks from his pack and slammed them together several times until a spark formed. Paul was standing close by with a piece of wood. After several tries and more sparks, almost instantly, the dry wood ignited, and they had a torch to see with.

Everything was black. The forms that resembled odd misshapen trees looked like they had been burned, but in fact, they were not. This is the way trees grew in the Black Forest. There were several leaves on each of these so-called trees. These leaves were also pitch-black in color.

In order to leave their hands free while in the Black Forest, it was agreed that only one torch would be lit. Not knowing what they would encounter, they didn't want to have to drop their lit torches and possibly start a forest fire in order to protect themselves from any unknown obstacles.

Larry held up the torch and took the lead with Carl, Rodney, and Paul following in a single file behind him. Even with the illumination given off by the torch, each of them stumbled occasionally, and the going forward was very slow and deliberate. A snake, black of course, slithered right across Larry's path. They all stopped and watched him disappear under a pile of black leaves. The air in the Black Forest did not have the sweet aroma of the forests in Alauria. Here, the air was thick and evil-smelling.

"What was that?" exclaimed Rodney, shaking his left arm sharply.

"Something is crawling up my leg. Both my legs!" said Paul.

"Larry, it looks like there is a spider on your shoulder," said Carl as he tried to knock the spider off Larry.

Black spiders in all shapes and sizes were surrounding the men. The floor of Black Forest was covered with them. Spiders hung by thin silky strands of web from the branches on both sides and above them.

As fast as the men were brushing the spiders off themselves, more spiders were landing on them from above, below, and right and left. The spiders were jumping from trees and running up their pants legs as if in a long-distance race.

"I can see a huge web-like structure in front of me!" said Larry, holding his torch up so they could all see it while brushing spiders off his chest and arms.

"Spiders don't like fire or flames. The extreme heat as well as the light will chase them away," said Paul. "Move your torch all around quickly, Larry."

Larry did as Paul advised, and the spiders scampered away from the men.

"It looks like the huge web is about ten feet high, and I can't see where the sides of the web ends. It goes on in both directions to the side as far as my light shows. It is like a large, sticky, silver wall," said Larry.

He thrust the torch in front of him igniting part of the large web. It started to melt as the flames spread along the strands up, down, and sideways. Spiders were jumping off the web and heading off into the Black Forest, out of sight. A five-foot section of the web rapidly melted away.

The men quickly walked through the burned and cleared web area. When they were about six feet past it, they turned. In the dim light afforded by their torch, they could see that the spiders were converging back on the damaged web and rebuilding it together in record time. Within two minutes, it was again a huge solid web with spiders crawling all over it. It again made a large silvery wall reflected in the torch light.

"Glad we got past that obstacle. I absolutely hate spiders," said Rodney.

"Me too!" added Paul.

"I'm not a friend of large black spiders either," said Carl.

"I like them as much as I like snakes, and you all know I do not like snakes," said Larry.

CHAPTER 10

They continued walking through the Black Forest for an uneventful two hours. It was thick with strange black undergrowth and smelled foul. Eerie unidentifiable sounds were periodically heard. Nothing would deter these men from their quest. They kept trudging onward thinking of rescuing Princess Charlotte as quickly as possible.

"Does anyone hear strange sounds coming from up ahead?" asked Carl.

The men stopped and tried to identify any unusual noise. "Yes. It is weird. It sounds like many ropes being pulled over the ground in all directions at once," said Paul.

"Let's proceed slowly and with caution until we can figure out what is making this sound," said Rodney.

"The floor of the forest stops abruptly about two feet in front of me," said Larry. "The torch doesn't show any trees or shapes of any kind in any direction except behind us."

"Lower the torch to your feet and look down," suggested Carl.

"Oh no," shouted Larry. "I can see hundreds of snakes slithering all over each other!"

"It looks like a canyon filled with black snakes of all sizes," said Carl looking over Larry's shoulder.

"Can you see any other sides to this pit?" asked Rodney.

Larry held the torch out over the perpetual motion of snakes and peered in all directions. "If I were to venture a guess, I would say the other side of this canyon is about fifteen feet ahead."

"I agree," said Rodney. "I can barely make out the outline of black branches of what must be trees on the other side."

"Can anyone see any edge to the right or left of this snake pit?" asked Paul.

Carl strained to see as Larry held the torch off to the right and then to the left. "Both sides seem never ending in this limited lighting."

"I guess the only way to get past these snakes is directly over the top to the other side," said Rodney.

Paul said, "Let's cut down as large a tree as we can find. We will put it across the pit from this side to the other side."

"We can't possibly walk across this snake-infested canyon without falling in," said Larry.

"I have an idea that should work. Trust me, men, I don't want to be snake dinner any more than the rest of you," said Paul.

After ten minutes of checking the nearest trees, they finally found one that seemed promising. It appeared to be about eighteen feet long and had a six-inch girth at the base narrowing to three inches at the top. They cut it down and stripped as many side branches off it as they could. Carl told them that he could probably manage to get the tree directly across the snake hole if Rodney and Paul would help hold it while Larry held the torch up high and as far across the pit as possible for Carl to see with.

Larry's estimate of fifteen feet across the pit was fairly accurate. Once in place, the tree stretched almost two feet past the pit on the other side.

Paul asked each man to give him their ropes. He joined them all together into one long piece. He then wrapped one end around his waist and tied it securely. He told Rodney to hold the rest of the rope and release it slowly, keeping it as taut as possible until Rodney reached the opposite side of the pit.

Paul instructed Carl to make sure the tree that now spanned the top of the pit did not move or turn while he crossed to the other side. He dropped to his knees and then began to slowly crawl across the entire length of the tree, hugging the tree tightly. Paul looked down and could see the writhing snakes only two feet below him. He was terrified of falling off this log. "Tell me that I'm not really crawling on a log over hundreds and hundreds of slithering snakes."

"You're halfway across, Paul. You are doing great!" said Larry who was leaning as far out over the pit as he dared in order to give Paul as much torchlight as possible to see his way.

Rodney was slowly releasing the rope to Paul as Paul inched forward. Carl was kneeling down in front of the tree on this side of the pit and holding the tree steady with every muscle he could.

"I made it!" shouted Paul with great relief while standing up on the opposite side. "Keep releasing more rope as I pull on it, Rodney."

Paul then felt in the darkness for a thick sturdy tree trunk. He found one about a foot from the edge of the pit. Paul proceeded to climb the tree. He untied the rope from his waist then secured it tightly to the tree. "Rodney, tie your end of the rope to as strong a tree trunk as you can find in a direct line from the log we laid across the pit. Tie it as firmly as you can about five feet off the ground keeping the rope as taut as possible."

Rodney did as Paul instructed. He then climbed down to the forest floor and joined Larry and Carl at the edge of the pit. "Do we have to do what I think we have to do?" asked Rodney.

"If you mean walk across the pit balancing on the log? The answer is yes," said Paul. "But now you have a rope to hold on to while crossing. The rope is high enough so that if you do slip off the log, you won't fall into the pit and become snake dinner."

"Rodney, you go first and show us how it is done," said Carl. "I will continue to hold the log steady while you and Larry cross."

Rodney gripped the rope with both his hands. The rope was just above his shoulders. He slowly proceeded across the pit looking down at the slithering mass of snakes directly below him. In less than five minutes, Rodney was safely across the pit. It was the longest five minutes in his entire life.

"Paul, Rodney, both of you move away from the edge of the pit. I am going to toss the torch across to you," said Larry. He pulled his right arm back and threw the torch in a high arc to the other side. It landed six inches from the edge of the pit. "Good show," said Rodney. "I'll hold it up for you, Larry."

Larry grabbed the rope with both hands and successfully edged his way across the pit. He did not look down at the snakes even once. He knew that if he looked down and saw them all writhing below him, he would probably freeze and not be able to move his feet any further toward the other side of this huge canyon of snakes.

"Okay, Carl. We will try to hold the tree steady while you cross," said Paul.

Carl released his hold on the tree, stood up, and grabbed the rope with both hands. He hoped that the tree below him would not roll or move out of position while he was crossing. Rodney stooped down to hold the tree as steady as he could while Carl was crossing. The part of the tree on this side was the skinnier top of the tree and not as sturdy as the trunk on the other side. Paul joined Rodney to try to hold the tree secure.

When Carl was about two feet short of the other side, the back of the tree moved. Paul and Rodney could no longer hold the tree in place.

"Jump now, Carl," shouted Rodney.

He and Paul quickly backed away from the tree to give Carl room to land safely. Carl immediately let go of the rope and sprung off the tree toward the edge of the pit. Just as he landed on the other side, the log fell onto the hundreds of snakes below. Larry leaned over the pit and held the torch out. The log could not be seen. Snakes had covered it immediately.

"That was close," exclaimed Rodney while helping Carl up off the forest floor. "Are you okay?"

"I'm fine, thanks," replied Carl.

There was absolutely no question or doubt that they would not find a way across the snake pit. Nothing would stand in the way of them finding Princess Charlotte and bringing her back home to King Stephen. No obstacle could exist that they would not overcome.

Paul untied the rope from the tree and asked the three of them to help him pull on the rope. All four of them pulled as hard as they could. The tree that the rope was anchored to on the other side of the pit snapped in two, releasing the rope. The rope end fell into the snake pit and was immediately covered with the writhing snakes. Slowly they pulled the rope out of the pit making sure there were no snakes coming up with the rope.

Paul untied the sections of rope and handed them back to the others. They may need the rope in the future. Who knew what else the Black Forest had in store for them.

CHAPTER 11

For the next two hours, they kept walking in as straight a line as possible from where they entered Black Forest. Paul, being the last in the procession, had marked a tree every ten feet or so in case they had to turn around, and so they could find their way back in the same direction they entered. If not, they may end up aimlessly wandering around Black Forest forever. He knew they would have to again get past the slithery snakes and creepy spiders if they were to head back in the same direction. Still it would be better to know what lay in their path than encountering any new unknown obstacles. The Black Forest had a reputation of being impossible to get through, and it was proving to be true.

The men heard strange sounds from unknown creatures, but they did not see any life form other than those horrid spiders and that terrible snake pit. There were no happy animal sounds in the Black Forest, only cruel, evil, scary noises. Carl imagined the army of ugly creatures all around them that the wizard was rumored to have at his beck and call. Who knows what the wizard was feeding to his army of protectors of the Black Forest. Those thoughts made Carl give an involuntary shudder.

At one point, they saw black liquid moving sluggishly from their right side to their left side. It looked thick and gooey but still moved. It was not stagnant but appeared to be a slow-moving black stream. "Since we do not know what this liquid consists of, I suggest we try to gather some wood, about six feet long, to make a bridge across this stream," said Larry.

Paul and Rodney reached out to their right and pulled on a tree nearest them. Carl tied a rope around the tree while Larry held the torch up high for them to see. It took three or four tries before the tree gave way and fell over. It was fifteen feet high and about nine inches in diameter. They maneuvered it across the black stream, and one at a time, they crossed to the other side. This tree was wide enough for them to keep their feet safely on it while walking. Larry crossed first. He turned and leaned forward holding the torch high over the bridge so the others could see and not lose their footing and fall into the black stream.

Throughout their walk in this almost total darkness, Rodney would pass wood to Carl so that Larry could ignite a new torch before his old one burned out. Carl then pushed the old torch firmly into the ground to extinguish its remaining embers until it afforded no chance of causing the forest to catch fire. The new torch was their only source of light in the solid darkness of Black Forest.

The strange sounds of creatures alien to the men continued to come from all around them. Even with their torch they did not see what made these eerie noises as they had such limited illumination.

"From the tales I heard years ago, we should be close to the middle of the Black Forest about now," announced Larry. "We have a choice to make. Should we try to get through the entire forest tonight or find a place to make camp and finish tomorrow?" he asked.

"Making a camping area and sleeping here is almost impossible. I think we should forge ahead no matter how late it gets," suggested Paul.

"I agree," added Rodney.

Carl, being anxious to find Princess Charlotte, voiced his opinion loudly: "Let's continue on and quickly."

"I too am anxious to get out of the Black Forest and rescue the princess," said Larry. "Then we are all in agreement to keep on forging ahead."

The men did not realize that maybe they spoke too quickly.

CHAPTER 12

Suddenly all noise stopped. There was complete silence around them. No creatures screamed or made any sound. It was eerie. A quick gust of wind came from out of nowhere and blew out their torch. They could see absolutely nothing. They could hear nothing.

Paul reached for Rodney's back. Rodney reached for Carl's at the same time that Carl touched Larry's back. Each acknowledged the touch, and therefore, they knew they were all still together.

Without any warning, a pair of red eyes glistened directly ahead of Larry. "Do you see that?" whispered Larry.

"Sure do," replied Carl quietly.

"What is it?" queried Rodney.

"I'm not sure I want to know," added Paul in a hushed voice.

The eyes floated above them and then whisked completely around them in a circle. Then, as if that weren't scary enough, a loud screech pierced the silence in the darkness. It seemed to come from all around them at once. There was no specific direction to identify from where it emanated.

"What are you doing in the Black Forest?" boomed a voice from somewhere in front of Larry. "This forest belongs to Baron Nelson of Grimalka and is protected by the great wizard Dreaddrick. Go back now or prepare to die!"

"Show yourself, you coward," yelled Paul in the direction of the voice.

In response, a swirl of gray light spun in a huge oval, and a human form began to appear directly in front of Larry. This was the source of the red glistening eyes. It wore a long black robe and had a tall pointed black hat on its head. The facial features were hard to distinguish, if indeed it were human and not animal. The gray light stream kept swirling around the form.

"I take it you are Dreaddrick," stated Larry.

"Leave! Now!" bellowed Dreaddrick. "Turn back immediately. You can go no further and stay alive!"

With that, he raised his right arm that appeared to be holding a wooden wand. He then struck his arm straight out in front of him and shouted a strange incantation. Immediately a ten-foot-long area of red hot searing, burning coals appeared directly before Larry. It continued to spread both left and right as far as they could see and to go on for an eternity. Dreaddrick disappeared with a *poof* precisely as the burning coals appeared. The red coals were the same glistening red as Dreaddrick's eyes.

Larry threw his now-dead torch onto the burning coals. It immediately caught fire and completely burned up in a matter of seconds.

"We can't make a wooden bridge across these hot coals," said Larry. "We need to find another way to cross this."

"Each of you, pass your empty water bags back to me," said Paul. "I have an idea that should work. Remember the black liquid stream we crossed a while back?"

"Of course! That's a perfect solution," said Larry, "But with one problem. How will we find it in this pitch blackness?"

"I have been marking our path since we entered the Black Forest," Paul proudly said.

Rodney asked for each man to pull out the ropes from their packs. "I will tie these ropes together to help Paul quickly find his way back to us."

After several minutes, Larry managed to tie his rope to Carl's. Carl, in turn, tied the other end of the rope to Rodney's. Then Rodney tied his rope to Paul's rope. Rodney then tied one end of the rope around his waist and said to Paul, "I will stand here with the rope tightly around me so you can find your way back. Tie the other end around your waist to leave your hands free to carry the bags. Signal when you are ready, and we will pull the rope and you back to us."

Paul tied the other end around his waist, gathered up the water bags, and felt the trees for the marks he placed on them. Several times he could not immediately find his mark, but eventually he did. It was slow going, but he finally found the black liquid stream.

Slowly Paul leaned over the wooden bridge they made and loaded up the water bags with the black liquid, careful not to let any of it drip on him. He put one bag over each shoulder to hang by their straps. The other two he held in each hand. Paul then yanked hard on the rope to signal to Rodney that he had filled the bags and was ready to return to them.

Rodney slowly pulled on the rope making it shorter between him and Paul. As the rope slackened quite a bit, Carl untied the pieces of rope and handed them to Larry, one rope segment at a time.

This worked out quite well as Paul was being pulled back toward Rodney his hands were free to hold the filled bags.

The only light they had now was the red glowing embers of coal in front of Larry. It wasn't much, but in the pure blackness around them, it was much better than nothing. By the time Paul finally arrived back to them, their eyes started to adjust to this little bit of illumination.

Paul passed the water bag from his left hand to Rodney who, in turn, passed it to Carl. Carl handed it on to Larry and said, "Be careful. We don't know what will happen if any of this gets on you as we don't have any idea what is in the back liquid," he reminded Larry.

Larry slowly poured the ingredients from the water bag onto the red burning coals by his feet. They heard a "hiss" and could vaguely see steam rise above it. After waiting a full thirty seconds, Larry announced, "It is working! When I empty this bag, pass up the next one."

Very slowly and deliberately, Larry poured the liquid in about a ten-inch-wide path directly in front of him. He continued going further into the burning coals. The first bag covered about two feet in length.

"It will probably take about ten minutes for the liquid to cool," he told the others. In the meantime, we must cut down a tree or two and lay it down on the cooled liquid for us to cross to the other side so we do not come into contact with either the coals or this strange liquid."

Rodney and Carl tackled the job of cutting down a small tree. They had to cut off all the branches and leaves, stripping the tree clean. The whole process was time consuming with the limited light they had to see with. By the time they finished, Larry was ready for them to pass the tree up to him. Slowly, Rodney, Carl, and Larry inched the tree onto the cooled liquid, being careful not to let the tree touch any live red burning coals. If the tree caught fire, they would have to start all over again.

After the tree was situated properly, Paul passed the next water bagful of black liquid to Rodney. Rodney handed it to Carl who waited until Larry walked on the tree to the other end before passing the bag to him. Larry slowly poured the liquid onto the red hot coals. He then walked back toward Carl and got off the tree. When the liquid cooled, they pushed the tree further up the now cool path. They continued performing the pour, cool, and move process until they ran out of liquid. Their bridge over the red hot coals ended about two feet short of the other side. The men all agreed that they could jump the final two feet without any problem, and they would not have to start over by tying the ropes together, getting the liquid, pouring it, cooling, and cutting down and completely trimming another tree.

Just as they were about to cross on their newly made bridge, Carl spotted something moving about on the other side about ten feet past the red coals. "Larry, what is that movement beyond the coals?" queried Carl loudly.

"It is difficult to see much further than the coals, but I too see something moving over there," added Larry. "In fact, there are two things moving, several feet apart."

"We have come this far. I suggest we continue crossing to the other side and tackle whatever it is when we get there," said Paul.

"I agree," Rodney put in. "We knew this quest was not going to be an easy one."

CHAPTER 13

Larry was the first across, followed shortly by Carl, then Paul and lastly, Rodney. The four of them stopped in front of the red burning coals to assess the motion ahead.

There were two cages about five feet apart. One had what appeared to be a white horse with a blanket over its back while the other cage encased the form of a man.

"Let's talk to the man but tread carefully as we do not know if he is friend or foe," cautioned Paul. The four of them slowly walked toward the smaller cage with the male figure in it.

"Why it's only a young lad," said Rodney who approached the cage first.

"Help us, please," begged the captured boy, "And hurry. The wizard, Dreaddrick, may reappear any moment."

In the darkness, it was difficult to see how to open the cage. Paul finally found a lock on the far side. "This is an easy one to break open," he said. "It will take a few minutes longer than usual in the dark, but we will have you free shortly."

As Paul was working on the lock, the boy told them he was fourteen years old. His name was Frankie, and he had been captured by Dreaddrick about a week ago. The wizard had seen Frankie and his silver horse playing in a field. He tossed a lasso at Silver with his magic rope but missed. Silver almost got away, but Dreaddrick threw his lasso over Silver again. His second attempt was successful. Unfortunately for Frankie, the wizard knew that special horses like Silver only obey their owner no matter what the consequences. Frankie was Silver's master.

"Silver is in the other cage. Please free him. He is very upset. He is not used to being caged in," said Frankie.

Rodney and Carl set about to open the lock to Silver's cage and bring him to Frankie.

"Take the blanket off Silver's back, and you will see why he is so special," said Frankie proudly.

After removing the lock and entering the cage, Carl carefully removed the blanket. He realized why this beautiful white horse was called "Silver" and knew that he, indeed, was truly special. Even though it was very dark, the red coals reflected off silver's sides giving more light to the area. Silver was a winged horse. They are magical. Winged horses can fly quickly and soar like birds. Silver's wings were a bright silver color. As soon as Carl removed the blanket, Silver flexed his wings slowly and turned his head to each side to check out his wings. He flapped them once or twice and then slowly walked over to Frankie with his head down. He nuzzled Frankie and then stood up tall and moved his front right hoof several times in the black dirt.

Frankie put his arms around Silver's neck in a big hug and gave him a kiss on the cheek. "I'm so glad you're all right, Silver," said Frankie softly. "We will go home now."

"First, I have to thank these men for saving us," said Frankie looking toward the men.

"What purpose did Dreaddrick have in keeping you both in cages?" asked Larry.

"Baron Nelson of Grimalka had a young lady with him, and they needed passage to his castle. He didn't want to risk taking her through the Black Forest because it is so dangerous. He sent Dreaddrick in search of a winged horse to fly them over the Black Forest," said Frankie.

"The wizard knew that winged horses only listen to their masters and won't fly for anyone else, so after Dreaddrick captured Silver, he cast a spell over me," said Frankie. "He warned me that if I didn't make Silver do as Baron Nelson wished, Dreaddrick would kill both Silver and me."

Frankie went on to say, "Baron Nelson and the beautiful lady climbed on Silver's back. He told me to have Silver fly them over the Black Forest to Grimalka Castle and then return to me. As soon as Silver came back, Dreaddrick threw his magic lasso over Silver again. Silver almost got away as Dreaddrick missed the first time, but his second attempt at lassoing Silver caught him just as all four of his legs left the ground. Holding onto the end of his magic rope, Dreaddrick forced us to fly after him from Alauria into the center of Black Forest. He kept us in the two cages until you freed us. Dreaddrick would magically appear once a day bearing apples and bucket of water for Silver and a few pieces of bread and goblet of water for me."

"Before you and Silver return home, would you help us?" asked Larry.

"Of course," replied Frankie. "You need only ask and anything in our power we will do for you."

"Ask Silver if he would fly the four of us to Castle Grimalka," said Larry. "You see, the young lady that was with Baron Nelson is Her Royal Highness Princess Charlotte of Alauria and the baron kidnapped her. We are on a quest to find the princess and return her safely to her father, King Stephen."

Frankie smiled, nodded, and turned to Silver. He whispered in Silver's ear and then said, "Silver is happy to help you. He can only handle two of you at one time, so he will make two trips."

Carl and Larry were the first to climb on Silver's back, both being very careful not to harm his beautiful silver wings. "Hold on tightly," called out Frankie to the men. Frankie then patted Silver on the nose, smiled, and said, "Hi-yo, Silver! Away!"

With that, Silver flapped his wings twice and then smoothly soared into the air, breaking through a black cloud hanging low over the Black Forest. He flew up straight through to the sun-filled sky above. Riding on Silver through the air was like riding on a horse on the ground, only much smoother, and way more exciting. It was exhilarating. The slow flapping of his silver wings reflecting the sun's rays and the cool breeze of the air passing by them while seeing the world down below from up above was magical. Carl would never forget this wonderful moment.

Carl looked down and saw how big the Black Forest really is. In the distance through the black clouds, Carl saw a forbidding-looking castle with black vines growing all around it. Silver headed right toward it. There were no colorful flowers or green grasses. No blue lakes with white swans gliding on the surface. Silver flew closer to the ground and slowed his speed. He gracefully put his wings straight up in the air and gently landed with all four hooves on the ground at once.

Immediately upon climbing off his back, Carl rushed to Silver's face, hugged him around the neck, and said, "Thank you, Silver."

Larry was only two steps behind Carl. He, too, thanked Silver and then patted him on the nose. Silver nodded in return and then took off back up in the air in the direction of the center of the Black Forest.

At least there were rays of sunlight coming through the gray clouds around Castle Grimalka. It was not as pitch-black as being in the Black Forest. Still, it was gloomy here. Everything had a grayish cast. This was not a happy land.

Moments later, Silver brought Rodney and Paul to where he let Carl and Larry down. After they dismounted the winged horse, Silver took off again, his silver wings glistening in the little sunlight that filtered through the gray clouds.

While the men were planning their next course of action, Silver and Frankie flew in.

"Do you need anything further from us now?" asked Frankie, walking over to Larry. Clearly he was anxious to return home. Both he and Silver had been through a terrible ordeal.

"No, but thank you for all you have done for us," said Larry. "We will contact you after we have returned Princess Charlotte to King Stephen."

Frankie climbed on Silver's back, and as Silver took off in flight, they circled over the men, and Frankie waved goodbye. Larry, Rodney, Carl, and Paul waved in return.

Now the men had to get on with their quest. There was no way to backtrack or obtain any additional assistance as the Black Forest lay between them and Alauria. They could only go straight forward to the castle. But the next step was going to be a difficult one because looking up at Castle Grimalka, one could not help but notice it was covered in thick black thorny vines that looked impossible to climb. And it was getting close to nightfall.

CHAPTER 14

"Where should we set up camp for the night?" queried Paul.

Larry pointed back toward the Black Forest and said, "Over there, by the big boulders. They should offer us some protection in the night from the Black Forest. We will take turns standing watch till morning."

As the men had not eaten since yesterday morning, Rodney set out scavenging for food. Paul and Larry decided to walk awhile and scout around the castle for any activity until Rodney returned. Carl was given the task of thinking up ways to scale the thorny vines as he was as close to an expert they had after he climbed over the hedges to Alauria. They agreed to meet back at the big boulders by the Black Forest before darkness fell.

Several hours later when they all gathered together, Rodney brought out a large backpack full of berries—black berries, of course. That was the only edible growth he could find.

Larry and Paul didn't have any good news. Although they didn't see anything moving at all in or around the castle, they couldn't see a viable way into it either. The thick black vines had large thorns every few inches and encompassed the entire base of the castle for at least thirty feet in height all around it.

"In addition to the vines, when we got closer to the castle, we discovered that there is a twelve-foot-wide moat around the entire building," said Larry.

"It was getting dark and we had to leave or we wouldn't have found our way back here easily, so we have no idea of what lives in the moat, if anything," said Paul. "So, after getting past the moat problem, we also have the thorny vines to tackle."

"I have several ideas of getting past the vine situation, but the mysterious moat could be a bigger problem," said Carl.

"I suggest we eat our blackberry dinner and then try to get as good a night's sleep as we can. We can brainstorm our next step in the morning," said Rodney.

"I'll take first watch," volunteered Carl, as he was not sleepy at all. He was worried about Princess Charlotte and what could happen to her if they couldn't save her from the evil Baron Nelson. Carl mused that it seemed every time they got a one step closer to completing their task of her rescue, they ran into another problem, each one more difficult than the preceding one.

Carl would walk one direction checking out the Black Forest to make sure there was no movement coming from there and then walked back in the other direction glancing toward the castle. There was a half-moon out and many stars, but they were mostly blocked by the dark gray clouds. Still, some light was better than none as they had found out while they were in the Black Forest.

After Larry relieved him and took over sentry duty several hours later, Carl lay on his back looking up at the few stars peeking out between the clouds and thought about tackling the moat. He fell asleep dreaming about all sorts of unimaginable creatures residing in the moat. It was a terrible nightmare. For each creature they found in the moat guarding the castle, one of them came up with a solution to get rid of it. Then another even worse creature would take the previous creature's place. This went on all night long in his fitful dreams. Carl was glad when morning broke and he arose because then he stopped dreaming about ugly, dangerous creatures.

For breakfast, they finished the supply of blackberries Rodney brought them the evening before. They packed up all their gear and sat in a semicircle on one of the huge boulders looking toward the castle.

"We'll tackle one problem at a time," suggested Larry. "The moat is the first one to conquer. We have to find out exactly what liquid the moat is comprised of. Then we will determine what may live in it. Lastly, we will figure out how and where to cross the moat to gain entrance to the castle."

"If we can discover where the drawbridge is that crosses the moat, maybe we can breach the castle without bothering with the moat," put in Paul. "The drawbridge is well hidden."

"We still should know what the liquid is and what lives in it in case we can't get out of the castle the same way we enter, providing of course that we enter through the drawbridge," said Larry.

They decided to walk toward the moat as they were carrying on their discussion. Rodney was the first to reach the moat. He exclaimed, "The liquid is not the black thick gooey mess that was in the Black Forest. This is gray and thinner. I can actually see down a few inches from the surface."

Paul pulled out the large walking stick he had picked up by the boulders. He thrust it into the moat. "Look!" he said excitedly. "I can only see three inches below the surface of the liquid. After that, the rest of the stick disappears and cannot be seen at all. The stick seems stuck, and I can't get it back out of the moat. It even seems to be pulling itself in deeper as I stand here."

"It must be quicksand," said Rodney as he put both his hands on the stick below Paul's to try to extricate the stick from the moat.

"There are snakes swimming in the moat, too" said Carl.

"Ooh, I do not like snakes," said Larry. "That black one in the Black Forest was bad enough; then the snake pit we had to cross. Now there are lots of snakes in this moat."

Swimming along in the top three inches of gray liquid were snakelike creatures. As they slithered around, one of them bumped into the stick, and for a few seconds light shone back at them. "Those things aren't snakes. They are electric eels," warned Paul.

"You're right, Paul," said Rodney. "And electric eels are worse than snakes."

"They are snakes that swim in water and pack a charge," added Larry. "They give a brief but painful numbing shock to humans."

"Imagine getting shocked by several of those eels at one time," said Rodney.

"Electric eels and quicksand are two reasons we should set aside the idea of crossing the moat right now," said Carl. "Let's concentrate on finding the drawbridge. Then we can decide what to do," he added.

Rodney and Carl were going to slowly walk around the castle to the left while Larry and Paul were to walk in the right direction. They decided that they would compare notes of what they found when the four of them met up again on the back side of the castle.

Four hours later, when they met on the other side of the castle, Rodney and Carl opened a pack and brought out blackberries for them to share for lunch. Rodney showed Carl where the blackberry bushes were and knew that they should get something to eat. Nothing else edible could be seen anywhere. While they ate, they discussed what they observed.

In comparing notes, they determined that the castle was about half the size of King Stephen's in Alauria. The walls around Castle Grimalka were about sixty feet high and seemed to be entirely comprised of large thick stone. There were ten turrets that could be seen from where they walked. Each turret had a gray flag with a single black rose in the center. Slim windows were scattered here and there in the upper part of the walls, but they were not large enough for any of them to fit through. They could only be used as defense to fire weapons through from inside the castle to the outside. None of them saw even an outline of a drawbridge in the walls. Every inch of the lower half of the walls was covered with thick black thorny vines. The moat, electric eels, and quicksand completely encompassed the castle.

"We *must* find a way to get inside those walls," groaned Carl feeling very frustrated.

So they decided to walk around the castle again. This time, all four of them would walk together. After half an hour, Carl noticed that there were two gray flags with a black rose in the center of each along the top wall line where there wasn't a turret. That was unusual. He stopped walking and stared up at them. Paul looked back at Carl and then followed the line of vision that seemed to consume Carl at that moment. He smiled and exclaimed, "Carl has found the location of the drawbridge."

"You're right, Paul. We just can't see it, but this must be the location," said Larry.

There was no other reason they could think of for the flags to be situated at that location. Now they had to figure out where the drawbridge was and how it worked. The black thick thorny vines kept the drawbridge chains well hidden.

That night, the men agreed to camp on the big boulders nearest these two flags so they could keep a watch on the area all night in case the drawbridge was lowered. This time, they slept two at a time while two kept their nightly vigil, one watching their surroundings and one watching only the castle drawbridge area.

Their careful vigil paid off. Several hours after darkness filled the sky the sound of heavy chains began to pierce through the night. Carl and Larry were on watch duty, but they didn't have to wake Paul and Rodney. The chains made so much noise it woke them up immediately. Two guards in black uniforms with gray stripes on their pants walked out of the castle across the drawbridge. One guard turned right and one turned left. Each one was carrying a large bucket. As they walked further apart, they turned and faced the moat and then tossed something into it.

"They're feeding the electric eels," exclaimed Paul.

"This is my chance," whispered Carl grabbing his gear taking off in a run, hunkering low. As soon as the guards feeding the electric eels, could no longer be seen, Carl quickly ran across the drawbridge and into the castle out of sight.

CHAPTER 15

Shortly after Carl slipped into the castle, the two guards returned from their mission. Apparently they had finished feeding the eels and were going back into the castle. The drawbridge was being pulled up again; their chains clunking loudly. There was no time for Larry, Rodney, or Paul to get into the castle unseen. If they attacked the two guards, more would come out looking for them. There was nothing they could do at that moment but hope that Carl had not been detected and was safe.

When dawn broke, the trio stood where the drawbridge had been last night, musing over what their next step would be. Now that they knew exactly where the chains were hidden behind the thick black thorny vines, they had identified an area of attack. They did not have the power to lower the drawbridge by the chains, but they now knew what lay behind that area in the castle—nothing. Where the rest of the walls were, there was no way of knowing if there was a roof, stairway, or any type of obstacle on the other side. Therefore, they were going to enter the castle at the location of the drawbridge.

Larry and Paul went a few feet into the Black Forest and cut down some tall thin trees that were on the very outside of the forest. While they were dragging the last two trees to the huge boulder that was their encampment area, Rodney was stripping the limbs and leaves off of the first tree.

Next, Paul and Larry cut down long black vines in the Black Forest and carried them to the stripped trees. Rodney then cut one tree into two foot sections. Larry and Paul wove the vines around the sections attaching them to the tallest stripped tree. The finished product was a crude but sturdy ladder, about thirty-five feet long.

They waited for an hour before nightfall. After dark, the people inside the castle would probably be inside their homes, and it would be harder for anyone to see them. The three men carried the ladder to the moat and slowly eased it against the castle wall to the top of the black thorny vine area directly below the flag on the right. Rodney climbed up the ladder carefully so as not to fall into the moat below. Larry had tied all their ropes together putting a loose noose at one end. He stood behind the ladder and tossed the rope up toward the flag above Rodney. It missed, and the end fell into the moat. Paul pulled the rope out of the moat and brought it to Larry to try again. On the third try, he was successful. Larry pulled the rope tightening the noose around the pole holding the gray flag with the black rose. Paul climbed up the ladder below Rodney and let the rope loosen until Rodney could reach it. Rodney then tied the rope around his waist, stood on the top rung, just above the thorny vines and climbed up the rope the last thirty feet of the wall to the flag pole. It was dark by the time he reached the top, so he was not seen by anyone. The walls were about two feet thick at this location. He untied the rope from his waist and slid the rope back down the outside wall where Larry, standing near the top of the ladder, caught the end. Rodney lay down on his stomach on the wall top while waiting for Larry to join him.

A few minutes later, Larry was on the top of the wall next to Rodney. He carefully threw the end of the rope back to Paul waiting on the ladder. Paul arrived shortly afterward. He had kicked the ladder down into the moat just as he stepped off the top rung. While hanging on to the rope wrapped around his waist, Paul looked down and watched their ladder slowly gurgle through the quicksand and disappear. Now there would not be evidence of anyone stealing into the castle. He untied the rope, coiled it up, and stowed it in his pack.

Rodney crawled along the top of the wall until reaching a tall roof. It was about twenty feet from where they scaled the wall. He quietly dropped down the three feet to the roof and signaled for Larry and Paul to follow. First, they had to find a place to obscure themselves from the people inside the castle. Second, they had to find Carl. And thirdly, and most importantly, they must find Princess Charlotte. Maybe Carl had already located the princess. At least all four of them were inside Castle Grimalka and much closer to rescuing the princess.

"Look over to the right and down about twenty feet. There's an open hallway that seems deserted," said Larry. "Let's head for that."

They climbed back up the wall to the top and slowly crept toward the hallway. About five feet before the hallway was an arch supported by a thick wooden post. There was a matching post on the on the other side of the arch. Paul reached it first and shimmied down the wooden post on the side closest to them. Larry followed right behind him. Rodney joined them in the hallway a few seconds later. Luck was on their side; the hallway truly was deserted.

CHAPTER 16

Carl had another lucky break when he crossed the drawbridge. The two guards that were on duty on the inside of the castle were busy flirting with two young girls and did not notice his entry. Since it was close to dark, and most people were headed toward their homes, he knew that no one would take much notice of another man in villager clothes walking toward the interior of the castle too.

Castle Grimalka was very similar to King Stephen's castle in that it had a large courtyard with two large wooden doors leading to the interior of the castle, except it was very gloomy here. Where Alauria's courtyard was filled with flowing fountains and beautiful sculptures in formal brightly colored flower beds of tulips, marigolds, and pansies, Grimalka had nothing but a few boulders. There were no carved topiaries in fanciful animal shapes like a unicorn, a fairy with delicate wings, a fire-breathing dragon, or a horse with wings like Silver. Everything here looked as gray as the castle walls. It was depressing and not happy here.

Carl passed through the open large wooden doors to the interior of the castle. Directly ahead of him were two more large wooden doors each with a black rose emblazoned on a gray shield. This, Carl surmised, must lead to Baron Nelson's throne room. A wide staircase rose off to his left leading up to a long gallery. "*That probably is where the royal bedchambers are*," thought Carl.

On Carl's right was an open archway that the citizens of Grimalka in plain villager clothing all walked through. Apparently, that was where the villager's homes were to be found.

Carl turned right and followed behind a group of villagers. The hallway behind the arch was only about thirty feet long. At the end was a huge open area surrounded by at least twenty doors on the ground level. Some of the walls were only eight feet high and appeared to be housing units for the villagers. Other walls were about twenty feet high and had balconies with stairs leading up to their doors. There were fifteen of these homes on the upper level. In the center of the open area stone tables and benches were scattered about. The only other items were a few large boulders, apparently serving no special purpose. They were just there. No colorful flowers or any statues adorned the open area. The house walls and the tables, benches, and boulders were the same gray stone that comprised the outer walls of Castle Grimalka. It was all very, very gloomy. The only light emanated from several lanterns, one hanging every twenty feet or so along the wall.

Carl knew that he could blend in with the villagers during the day, but he had to find a place to hide away while he learned the layout of the rest of the castle. He was pretty sure that Princess Charlotte was being held captive upstairs in the bedchamber area accessed by the stairway he noticed upon entering the inner castle walls.

All of a sudden, someone yanked his jacket on his lower right arm. Carl turned quickly and looked down at a small boy of about seven years old with honey colored hair and large clear blue eyes. He looked up at Carl and said in a small voice, "I don't know you."

Carl said the first thing that came to his mind. "I usually work in the stables. I haven't seen you around there." He thought that was a safe reply as most little boys do not hang around the stable areas.

"I'm not allowed to play near the horses. My name is Jake. What's your name?"

"I am known as Will," replied Carl as he smiled at the little boy. Carl didn't exactly know why he made up a name rather than tell the boy he was Carl, but he had a feeling that it was wiser to hide his identity and purpose for being here right now.

"Wanna play hoops?" asked Jake hopefully.

"It's almost dark, and the lanterns don't give off enough light to play hoops now," answered Carl.

"Jaaaaake. Come in, boy," someone called out from one of the open doors along the upper living quarters.

"Coming," Jake yelled in response.

Jake then grabbed Carl's hand and pulled him along as he walked in the direction of a stairway that led to the upper doors. "My brother Billy and I play marbles right after dinner. Play with us, Will."

Spying Jake as he was almost at the top of the stairs, a woman told Jake to hurry. She added, "And bring along your friend." She couldn't see how tall Carl was as he was several stairs behind Jake, and she could only see the top of a head.

Upon crossing the threshold of the door that the woman disappeared behind, Carl saw a tall, thin, young woman with long hair bending over and stirring a pot of what looked like soup. The pot was hooked to a piece of metal supported by a tripod hanging over a small open fire in the center of the room. There were three straw mats along the far wall and a table with two benches against the wall on the right. Along the left wall was a small plain wooden chest of drawers with a large bowl and jug sitting on top. The room was very sparsely furnished but clean. A small boy about five years old with a shock of red hair and the same large clear blue eyes as Jake's was lying on top of one of the straw mats. When the woman stopped stirring the soup and brought the pot to the table, she looked Carl up and down and said, "I thought that Jake was playing with one of his friends."

"Will *is* a friend, Mama," said Jake. "Can he play marbles with Billy and me after dinner?" he asked.

"I guess one more won't matter," his mother replied. Turning to Carl she said, "You can help by carrying Billy to the table." She nodded to the boy lying on the mat.

"Billy can't walk so he can't play hoops with me, but he is real good at marbles," said Jake.

Carl walked over to Billy, bent over, and gently picked him up. He carried him to one of the benches by the table and carefully set him down. The table was set for three, so Jake's mother quickly put another bowl and spoon on the table for Carl.

Jake sat down on the bench opposite Billy and patted it, telling Carl to join him there. Jake's mother sat down next to Billy. Carl noted that Jake and his mother shared the same honey-colored hair and that Jake, Billy, and the mom all had matching large clear blue eyes.

While eating the soup, Jake's mom said her name was Lily and asked Carl about himself. She too hadn't seen him around. Jake immediately said that "Will" worked in the stables.

"That explains it," said Lily. "I work in the bedchambers in the castle, and the little spare time I have, I am here in the castle grounds tending to Billy. The stables are a long way off from the castle," she added.

After supping, Carl carried Billy to the straw mat. Jake brought his marbles over to them and laid them on the floor in front of Billy. He told "Will" to sit down so they could play. The three of them played marbles while Lily rinsed the dishes and spoons in the large bowl on top of the chest of drawers.

"Time for bed, boys," announced Lily.

Billy lay down on the straw mat he was sitting on while playing marbles. Jake told his mother that he would sleep next to Billy so that Will could sleep on his mat.

"Since the stables are a long way off, and it is late, Jake is right, Will. You can sleep on his mat tonight if you like," suggested Lily.

This was ideal as Carl had no place to sleep for the night. He thanked Lily and got ready to spend the night on Jake's mat.

CHAPTER 17

Larry, Rodney, and Paul stood in the empty stone hallway taking in their surroundings. The hallway was about sixty feet long and appeared to have at least twenty large wooden doors, ten on each side. The hallway was well illuminated as candlelit lanterns lined both walls, one on each side of every door. As they walked forward in the direction of the end of the hallway, they noticed gray tapestries with one single black rose on each one hanging on the walls between every set of doors. At the end of the hallway was a gallery with an open area below.

Instead of the gallery being open to a library as in Castle Alauria, this one overlooked a great dining hall. There was one oversized thick wooden table thirty feet long stretching along the far end of the room with intricately carved chairs lining the back length of the table. Along each side wall were several smaller tables with benches on both front and back, each table seating approximately twenty-five people. The center of the gray stone floor was inlaid with a huge black stone rose.

Directly opposite where this hallway ended was another hall-way that was larger in width than this hallway with grander lanterns adorning the walls. Apparently that hallway was for the royal bed-chambers, and this hallway was for the bedchambers of lesser import-ant personages.

As they were gazing over the gallery rails to the dining hall below, activity started. Servants were bringing in plates and goblets and laying them out on the tables. Evidently, preparations for the evening meal had just begun.

"We look out of place up here. We dare not be seen roaming these hallways dressed in villager garb," proclaimed Larry.

"I noticed that the opposite end of the hallway we just walked through had stairs to the ground level leading to the castle courtyard by the drawbridge," said Rodney.

"Let us hurry and get out of here now," said Larry.

Just then, a door opened about fifteen feet from where they were standing and between the men and the stairs. They quickly moved to the gallery area, turned right, and pressed against the wall. Two men dressed in black finery with gray fur trim walked down the hall in the direction of the gallery. Luckily for Larry, Paul, and Rodney, as the two men reached the end of the hall, they turned to the left and continued to walk around the gallery toward the royal bedchambers.

As soon as the two men who had turned passed them and entered the royal bedchamber area, Larry, Rodney, and Paul scooted to the now-empty hallway and rushed to the stairs leading to the courtyard. They raced down the stairs and stood behind the nearest boulder. Their timing was perfect because many more doors began to open, and people poured out into the hallway upstairs heading for the gallery and the dining hall below.

"Until we can find a secure place to hide for the evening, we must find a way to blend in around here," said Larry.

"First, we should hide our swords as villagers do not ordinarily carry them," said Paul. He put his hand out for Larry and Rodney to pass over their swords to him. He then put all four swords behind a set of large boulders in the courtyard. Paul had brought Carl's sword with him as Carl did not have time to bring his sword along with his other gear when he sneaked into the castle last night.

"I smell the aroma of dinner cooking coming from someplace on our right, and I'm getting hungry," said Rodney, thinking about their last few meals consisting of a few handfuls of blackberries.

"Maybe we could go to the kitchens and act as servers or cooks," added Paul.

"Let's try. But we should go in one at a time to be on the safe side," cautioned Larry.

Larry strode off in the direction of the cooking smells and disappeared behind a small door in the wall. When he opened the door, he saw six huge fireplaces, big enough to walk in taking up the entire right wall. There were many pots hanging from metal hooks over the fires. Dozens of pots and pans as well as assorted cooking utensils hung from hooks over the food preparation tables in the middle of the room. Six ovens lined the opposite wall. He smelled pork, goose, fowl, and beef simmering in various sauces. Cooks were chopping vegetables in large piles and putting them into huge kettles. When one kettle was full, two men would bring the kettle to a hook over one of the fireplaces. Activity was going on all around him.

Seeing him standing there and not doing anything, a big burly man with a mustache and beard grabbed Larry's hand and put a knife in it and said, "Here you go. Peel and cut up those potatoes." The man pointed to a four-foot-high barrel with potatoes spilling out over the top. "When you have finished them, start on the carrots in that second barrel. Scrape the peelings off your worktable into one of the empty barrels."

Larry immediately grabbed a bowl sitting on the shelf above the potato barrel and filled it with potatoes. He brought it back to the table and started peeling and then cutting the potatoes into large chunks.

As Larry started on his second bowl, Rodney entered the kitchen. He looked at Larry and smiled. He never thought he'd see "Lord" Lawrence peeling potatoes. The smile didn't last long because the bearded man, who they later learned was named Frederick and who had commandeered Larry to peel potatoes, yelled at Rodney to "get a move on and stir the soup." He nodded to the set of pots in the second fireplace.

Rodney put his hands on the oversized ladle sticking out of the soup pot and began to stir. This time, Larry looked at "Sir" Rodney, and it was his turn to chuckle.

"Also, help Helena knead the loaves of bread and put them in the ovens. Hurry! The breads don't make themselves!" roared Frederick at Rodney.

Paul wasn't as lucky as Larry and Rodney. When he entered the kitchen, he was grabbed by a very fat woman and dragged to the far end of the kitchen. His job was to wash the dishes as they were brought back from the dining hall. While waiting for the dirty dishes to be brought into the kitchen, he was told to carry the garbage bins to the outside door so the animals could be fed. These bins were larger than the vegetable barrels. There were nine barrels already full and ready to be removed. Each weighed at least sixty pounds.

The trio worked in the kitchen all through the dinner and had to clean up the kitchen after the festivities were over, well past midnight. They were exhausted, but they managed to eat a hearty meal while working. Before Paul was allowed to leave for the night, he was instructed to take all the bins he put outside for the animals over to the stables.

"There are two carts and a wheelbarrow out there already. Fill them with the barrels and take the tunnel to the stables. When you have finished, you can get some sleep. Just be back here at day-break to work on breakfast for the baron and his friends," instructed Frederick.

"Larry, Rodney, come help me," called out Paul. He told them what he was directed to do. Elated to hear that there was a tunnel to the stables that was not in the castle but off somewhere on the grounds, they were delighted to help Paul. This could be another way in and out of the castle, if needed. It also may provide them with sleeping accommodations.

The information about a tunnel came at a big price for them. The barrels were heavy, and there were seventeen of them in all. They managed to put four barrels on one cart and two smaller barrels in the wheelbarrow. After both carts and the wheelbarrow were filled and the barrels anchored down, they had to look for the tunnel entrance. They searched the entire courtyard for ten minutes and couldn't find it.

"Why haven't you brought the barrels to the stables yet?" bel-lowed Frederick while coming out of the kitchen.

"Just about to bring the first batch," replied Paul.

"Then why are you standing over here and not by the tunnel entrance?" Frederick said crossly to Paul. "It's behind the boulder to your right!"

Larry pulled one cart toward the boulder while Rodney pulled the other cart. Paul had already pushed the wheelbarrow behind the boulder and found the entrance to the tunnel. It was well hidden from eyesight. He looked in the tunnel, but there were no lanterns in there. Paul looked around and saw several torches lying on the ground near the tunnel entrance. He picked one up and took it to one of the many glowing lanterns lining the wall by the kitchen and lit the torch. Larry and Rodney followed suit. They then wedged the torches between the barrels on the carts and in the wheelbarrow so they would have light in the tunnel.

The men pushed and pulled their conveyances the whole dis-tance to the stables. It took approximately ten minutes. The tunnel was comprised of gray stone walls, ceiling, and floor. It was about twelve feet high and ten feet wide. The double doors at the other end were open, and the stable hands were waiting for them.

The stable area was well lit with lanterns all around. Not only were horses in the stables, there was a pen with pigs on one side of the stable with a fenced-in area with sheep next to that. Behind the pigpen was a hen house and also a corral filled with steers. Beyond the corral was a large tract of land filled with vegetables. Larry mused that this enormous garden must be the source of produce for the kitchens.

"After you bring the rest of the barrels from the kitchen and the animals are fed, you can sleep on the straw mats behind the stables," instructed Hans, one of the stable hands, upon seeing the men emerge from the tunnel. "Andrew and I will empty the barrels, feed the animals, and take the empty barrels to the gardens to be filled by the gardeners. In the morning, you can bring the barrels that are full of eggs and vegetables to the kitchens with you," he said while pushing a lock of his sandy-colored hair away from his eyes. Hans was about twenty years old, very young for such an important position in the stables, but he had a very quick mind. His alert grayish blue eyes didn't miss anything. He made up in mental alertness for his medium height. He also was very muscular, which he had to be in order to move these heavy barrels around the stable areas.

Larry, Rodney, and Paul took two more trips pushing and pulling the carts and wheelbarrow though the tunnel to the stables. It was after two in the morning by the time all of them fell asleep, completely exhausted, on the straw mats.

CHAPTER 18

Carl awoke in the morning to the wonderful aroma of eggs and bacon cooking.

While Lily set the table for breakfast, she said, "Jake will take you to the kitchens. The kitchen is as far as he is allowed to go. The stables are too dangerous for a small child to play in," she cautioned.

Carl picked up Billy and brought him to the table and set him down on the bench.

"Promise me, Will, that you will not let Jake go to the stables," pleaded Lily while slicing bread and placing it in front of Carl's plate.

"Mom won't let me near the stables. That's where Billy got hurt and lost the use of his legs," said Jake. "I'll tell you the whole story later when you come back to play hoops with me."

After breakfast was finished, Carl carried Billy down the stairs to the courtyard and set him down on a stone bench where he was met by several friends. Jake and Carl walked around the inner castle courtyard to the kitchens. They had to maneuver themselves among the cooks and workers in the bustling kitchen to arrive at the back door by the garbage bins. Halfway through the kitchen, Carl spied Larry cutting up ham for bacon. Then he saw Paul pouring mead into goblets stacked on trays on a side table. Paul looked at Carl, smiled and nodded toward Rodney, at the back of the kitchen washing up the dishes.

"Come on, Will," cried out Jake pulling on Carl's arm. "It's too hot in here. Let's get going."

Rodney was watching Carl and Jake and heard what Jake said to Carl. He carefully made sure not to call him "Carl."

Rodney said, "Will, wait outside in the kitchen bin area and help me load up the food barrels that have to be brought to the stables."

"Who's your friend, Will?" asked Jake.

"Someone I have to help with his work in the kitchens. You go back home now, Jake. I'll see you later, and we'll play hoops," said Carl to Jake. "Besides, I promised your mother I wouldn't let you go past the kitchens or anyplace near the stables."

"Ohhh, okay," said Jake clearly disappointed that he could go no further than the kitchens. He slowly threaded his way back through the kitchen to the castle courtyard door. Carl watched Jake leave, and when Jake turned around at the kitchen door, he smiled and waved to Carl. Carl returned his smile and waved back to Jake.

Rodney immediately dried his hands on a towel hanging on a hook in front of him and walked to the back door with Carl. "Wait here outside the door. Larry, Paul, and I will be out after breakfast is finished in the dining room. We'll take you to the stables through the *tunnel*," said Rodney happily.

"Great," replied Carl with a broad grin. "*Tunnel, that's interesting*," thought Carl to himself.

As Rodney was walking back into the kitchen, he turned to Carl and said questioningly, "Will?"

"I'll explain later," replied Carl.

Carl began to walk around the back courtyard by the kitchen doors. He saw the kitchen carts and wheelbarrows, but no sign of a stable or a tunnel leading to it. Carl walked around the courtyard for almost an hour but only saw the inner castle walls and the outer castle walls and lots of large boulders.

"The entrance to the tunnel is well hidden," said Rodney walking up to Carl. "Help me put some of these barrels onto one of the kitchen carts. Larry and Paul will be here shortly, and we will go through the tunnel to the stables."

The breakfast barrels were far fewer than the dinner barrels, and with four of them working together instead of three, it only took two trips through the tunnel to the stables. Carl stayed in the stable area after the first trip while Larry, Paul, and Rodney finished transporting the rest of the barrels to the stables.

"Hans has been showing me all around this compound," exclaimed Carl when Larry, Paul, and Rodney joined him, their tasks completed for the morning.

"Carl has volunteered to work in the stables today," said Hans after Carl introduced them all to each other.

"I'll go back to the kitchens to help you bring the dinner barrels back later. Hans has been very helpful in telling me how the castle works with the stables," Carl told Larry.

"The reason for the long tunnel between the kitchens and the stables is because the stables and gardens are in a small valley, and the Near-Dead Swamp lies above the ground between them. It is hard to see the swamp unless you climb up on the boulders," Carl told Larry, Paul, and Rodney.

The four of them climbed the nearest set of boulders, and when they got to the top, they saw a swamp that stretched both left and right as far as they could see. Directly ahead of them, they could see only the turrets of Castle Grimalka. Below the turrets, the only sight was cypress trees, draped with Spanish moss, both dark gray in color. It was all very grim.

"Hans warned that most of Near-Dead Swamp is quicksand and too dangerous to attempt to cross. The outer walls of the castle cannot even be seen from here with all the cypress trees in the swamp," explained Carl.

"So when we walked behind the castle, we didn't see the swamp because it was behind the huge boulders quite a distance from the thick thorny walls and the moat," said Paul.

"Right," said Carl.

"I suppose that when the baron requires horses, they are brought through the tunnel and around to the courtyard by the drawbridge," said Larry.

"Right again," said Carl.

Larry, Rodney, and Paul returned to the kitchens and agreed to meet Carl after the dinner meal was over to discuss what to do next.

Carl worked with Hans and several other stable hands until after lunch. He learned where everything was and what everyone did at the stables before he left.

"I'll be back later tonight," he told Hans as he entered the tunnel.

CHAPTER 19

While Larry, Paul, and Rodney were working in the kitchens and dinner was being served in the great dining hall, Carl decided to search for Princess Charlotte. He climbed the stairs Larry told him they used to gain access to the upper hallway.

Carl walked down the hallway to the gallery and looked over the railing at the revelers in the dining room. He first checked out the main table. Seated at the very center was a well-clothed man with black hair, mustache, and goatee. He was dressed all in black—a black cotton top and pants with black fur trim. He wore a large pin on the left front of his jacket with what appeared to have a gray background with a black rose in the center, matching that of the stonework in the center of the room. He was flanked by two men who wore matching black suits with gray fur trim. The rest of the people at the main table were all dressed in varying shades of gray, black, and dark brown. When Carl looked at the other tables, all the diners were clad in dark somber colors. No one was wearing bright colors like red, green, yellow, or blue. In fact, even the walls were bare gray stone. No colorful flowers adorned any tables.

Each diner had a plate full of meats, fruit, breads, and vegetables of all kinds in front of them. That was the only color in the room besides their goblets. The main table had golden goblets while the lesser tables were adorned with silver goblets. There were no musicians or entertainment of any sort. The only sound in the hall was the loud talking among the diners.

Not seeing a trace of Princess Charlotte anywhere in the great dining hall, Carl quickly walked to what appeared to be the bedchamber hallway for the nobility. The only sign of life he saw were two royal guards standing outside the second door on the left. Carl surmised that that was where Princess Charlotte was being held captive. While pondering what to do to gain access to the room, luck came his way. Two servant girls approached the guards. Each servant was carrying a tray with food and drinks on it. They handed the trays to the guards. The guards started talking with the servants and began walking away from the door where they were standing sentry duty. One of the girls opened a nearby door and signaled for the guards to bring their trays. The four of them disappeared into a room leaving the door open, and Carl could hear them talking and eating.

Carl immediately rushed to the now unguarded door. The key was in the lock. He carefully turned the key unlocking the door and quietly opened it. Carl held his breath as his eyes landed on the beautiful girl of his visions.

The princess was seated on a black velvet settee in front of the fireplace. Even though she was no longer clad in the bright blue gown, now wearing a plain black silk dress, she was still the most beautiful sight he had ever seen. Her long golden tresses shone even brighter, if possible, against the blackness of the room reflecting the gold and red flames of the roaring fire and the candlelit chandelier.

The room was draped all in black. The coverlet on the bed was black and was adorned with a black rose embroidered in the center of a gray square. A large carved chest of drawers was against the wall next to the door and had a bowl and pitcher sitting on top. A small window was partially obscured with a long black curtain in the center and heavy black drapes on each side. A circular gray rug with a black rose lay on the floor in the middle of the room. From the ceiling hung a two-foot-wide chandelier with two dozen lit candles.

As Princess Charlotte turned her head to see who entered her chambers, Carl put his finger to his mouth to signal her not to make a sound. She immediately knew he was not an enemy as he was wearing villager clothing and not a royal guard uniform.

Carl rushed over to her, got down on one knee, and said, "Princess Charlotte, my name is Carl and your father, King Stephen, has sent me along with Lord Lawrence, Sir Rodney, and Sir Paul to bring you home."

The princess smiled widely and said in a soft voice, "Thank you, Carl."

Carl's heart melted at those simple words from this beautiful vision. But he knew that now was not the time to say anything except, "We will return shortly and whisk you away from Baron Nelson. Have no fear."

He knew that time was limited, so he got off his knee, and while he stood, Carl reached into his vest pocket and took out his mother's locket. As he handed it to the princess, he said, "Take this, and every time you feel afraid, just look at the locket and know that we will be back soon and take you home to safety."

Princess Charlotte stood and reached out for his arm. At her light touch, Carl turned and then the princess stood on her toes and kissed his cheek. Carl smiled, turned back toward the hallway, rushed out of the room, and quickly closed the door. He was glad the princess did not see him blush. Carl relocked the bedchamber door. He slipped the door key into his vest pocket as he ran down the hallway toward the gallery. When Carl turned into the hallway toward the courtyard stairs, he realized he managed to leave just in time. As he looked back, he saw the two royal guards wiping the last vestiges of dinner from their mouths while closing the door to their room. The servant girls were carrying the trays and walking down the hallway away from the guards.

Carl reached the kitchens as Larry, Rodney, and Paul were all just finishing up their cooking chores for the evening.

"I have good news!" exclaimed Carl to Larry.

"We can't talk now. We will be ready to leave in about an hour. Tell us all then, Carl," said Larry.

As Carl walked past Paul, he said, "Let us meet by the tunnel entrance."

CHAPTER 20

When Rodney finally came out from the kitchen, he caught Carl's eye and motioned for him to help him with the barrels. While Rodney and Carl were loading up the second cart, Larry and Paul emerged from the kitchen and began to load two barrels into the wheelbarrow. Since it was past midnight, the courtyard was fairly well lit with the wall lanterns. Carl found four torches, lit them from the lanterns, and handed one to each of the men. They anchored the lanterns on the barrels and began their trek through the tunnel to the stable area.

Again, since there were four of them, it only took two trips to bring all the barrels to the stables. Carl was anxious to relay his meeting with the princess to the men, but it was difficult to talk while pulling the heavy loads. The minute they finished unloading the barrels, Carl started talking as fast as he could. As he talked, he put his hand in his vest pocket and pulled out the key to the princess's bedchamber. He fully detailed his entire adventure, except for the kiss on his cheek by the beautiful princess.

"We know that we can gain access to the quarters where they are holding her captive while the guards dine. They don't like to eat standing up but rather sitting down and enjoying the company of the female servants in the room next door. But it is less than ten minutes that they are gone from guarding the door," explained Carl worriedly. "And they leave the door of the room they are dining in wide open."

"It seems our best time to rescue the princess will be during the dinner hour. The morning guards may eat their breakfast before their tour of duty outside her door begins. We don't know their routine," said Larry.

"We know when and how we can take the princess out of her bedchambers, but we need to plan the escape route first," said Paul.

"Hans has shown me all the horses in the stables and where the saddles are hung. We need four fast steeds and four saddles," said Carl.

"No, we need five saddled horses. The princess is an excellent horsewoman," said Larry.

"Princess Charlotte is as good in the saddle as our best jousters and swordsmen," added Rodney.

"Well then, we must leave our kitchen duties early tomorrow evening, just as the baron starts to dine. That will give us a good hour to reach the princess's bedchambers and bring her down to the drawbridge courtyard unseen," said Larry.

"I will tell Hans that I will take the evening chores of feeding the horses and tell him to go to bed early," said Carl.

"Carl, you will definitely need help in getting five horses saddled and brought through the tunnel. We will come to the stables and help you," said Paul.

"Rodney can wait with the saddled horses in the courtyard while the rest of us fetch the princess," said Larry.

"While we mount the steeds, what about the royal guards on sentry duty at the drawbridge?" asked Rodney. "Every time we go to the kitchens, there are at least two and sometimes four guards, two on each side of the drawbridge gates."

"It also takes two men to let a drawbridge down. It took almost two minutes for the drawbridge to be fully lowered once we heard the chains the night that the guards fed the electric eels," said Paul.

"Paul is our best swordsman, and Rodney is our champion jouster. They will ride first toward the drawbridge," said Larry.

"Rodney and I can take out two guards each without any problem," said Paul.

"Carl can ride directly behind us, dismount, and one of us will help him lower the drawbridge. Larry will have to stay behind with the princess to ensure her safety since he is an excellent swordsman," said Rodney.

"We should be able to rescue Princess Charlotte, run down the hallway and stairs, mount up, remove the guards, and lower the drawbridge within ten minutes," declared Larry. "If all goes as planned," he added.

Having laid out their plans for tomorrow evening's adventure, the men went to their straw mats and had their first good night's sleep in many days.

CHAPTER 21

Larry, Rodney, and Paul walked through the tunnel to the kitchens well before dawn to begin their chores for the day. They wanted to make everything seem like normal before they took off to save the princess.

Immediately after breakfast, Carl decided to find Jake. He had promised to play hoops with him. Carl also wanted to say goodbye to Billy and thank Lily for her kindness in feeding him and letting him stay with them the first night he was in the castle grounds.

Jake was playing in the courtyard with two other small boys. Upon seeing Carl approach, he smiled at him and waved. While Jake ran from his friends and over to Carl, he said, almost out of breath, "Will, are you going to play hoops with me now?"

"That's why I am here, Jake," said Carl smiling.

They played hoops in the courtyard for almost an hour. Several of the other villager boys joined in on the fun with them. Carl finally said he was tired and wanted to stop for a while. He asked Jake where Billy was this morning.

"He wasn't feeling well, so he is still lying on his straw mat," answered Jake.

They walked up the stairs to Jake's home to talk with Billy.

Billy was sleeping soundly, and they thought it better not to disturb him. Jake said, "Billy used to be so much fun before his accident."

"What happened? You said you would tell me the whole story," said Carl.

"It was about a year ago. We were playing marbles at the stables while our father was milking the cows. Jake and I were sitting on the ground in the courtyard near the stable doors. Baron Nelson and his wizard, Dreaddrick, had just come through the tunnel and entered the stables. The wizard is scary. Everyone is afraid of him, even the horses. Dreaddrick had opened one of the stall doors to examine the horse inside. The horse reared back in fear and then suddenly rushed forward and out through the stall and the stable. He ran right for us. I stood up in time, but Billy didn't. The horse trampled over Billy, crushing his legs, and continued running off. Billy hasn't been able to walk since," explained Jake. He lowered his head, clearly very upset.

"We are not allowed anywhere near the stables since Billy got hurt. Our father had immediately rushed to Billy, and when he tried to pick him up, Dreaddrick being so angry that the horse took off, pulled out his wand. He was trying to zap the horse, but he hit our father instead. F-f-f-father died right there and then," cried Jake. Tears then flooded out of his eyes and down his face.

Carl immediately put his arms around him and tried to comfort Jake holding him closely. After several minutes, Jake wiped away his tears and stood up saying, "Billy is awake, Will. Let's play marbles with him."

As Jake was trying to put up a big brave face in front of Billy, Carl agreed to play marbles with them. They played happily for almost an hour.

Then Lily burst through the door. Very excitedly, she proclaimed, "Baron Nelson has declared today a special day. He is to marry the princess from Alauria this evening, and we are all to make preparations for the celebration."

Carl could not believe what he just heard. "Tell me all, Lily," he demanded.

"Everyone is happy that there will be a big party but unhappy that that poor beautiful lady will be married to the evil baron," she explained. "She seems very sad too. The princess spends most of the time standing by the windowsill and gazing far off," added Lily.

Lily walked to the door and said, "I have to rush. Every man, woman, and child is to work on the preparations. Since I have been working in the royal bedchambers, my job will be to clean everything in the room for the princess, except the gown the baron had ordered made especially for this occasion. The seamstresses are still working on the dress. Everything must be spotless. Jake, you and Billy are to go to the courtyard and work on the streamers."

"What time are the nuptials?" asked Carl.

"At dinner time."

"Where will the wedding happen?" asked Carl.

"It will be held in the great dining hall. I really must get back. I just came here to tell the boys to get to work on the festivities," replied Lily.

"Can I help you in the chambers?" eagerly asked Carl.

"No," replied Lily as she walked through the door. Lily then stopped and turned toward Carl. "Well, maybe," she added thoughtfully.

"I will do anything. Tell me what I can do," Carl pressed.

"The curtains and drapes as well as the duster on top of the four-poster bed are all anchored up high in the room, and it is difficult for me to reach them easily," said Lily. "If you don't mind, you can take them down for me and put them back up when I finish cleaning them."

"Of course," replied Carl hurriedly.

"Jake, rush down to the kitchens and tell the man I was talking to yesterday that 'Will is assisting your mother in cleaning the princess's bedchambers.' I am sure they already have heard the news about the upcoming nuptials," said Carl.

CHAPTER 22

While Jake rushed off to tell Rodney what Carl asked, Carl picked up Billy and carried him downstairs to the courtyard. The men and women and children had already begun working on streamers and other items in preparation for the nuptials. Carl sat Billy on a bench where other children were assembling gray flags with a black rose in the center of each to a thin rope.

He then looked for Lily who was impatiently waiting for Carl at the bottom of the stairs leading to the upper hallway. She was tapping her foot and fretting that she was late.

Carl said, "Relax, Lily. Tell them that you had to find a strong man to do the heavy work, and everyone was already busy with preparations."

Lily relaxed at having an explanation for being late and threw a relieved smile toward Carl as they climbed the stairs.

People were bustling around this way and that. As they passed by open doors, they heard, "What gown should I wear tonight?" from one room.

"Tell that wretch of a maid that I want my hair combed and pinned *now!*" said someone from another.

"The baron is seating us at the back of the room. I won't stand for that! Tell his right hand that we *must* be seated in front!" someone said from still another room.

"Oh, dear, my dress is torn. Send for a servant immediately!" a voice came out of another doorway.

"Here are your pearls, my dear," said a man while entering a room on the left. He had just rushed past them in the hall and was carrying a black velvet case out in front of him.

"You can't wear that! You've gotten so fat your buttons are popping off!" was heard through a closed door on the right.

"These shoes are the only ones that match my gown, but they don't fit anymore!" was yelled through the closed door on their left. They heard a loud "thump" right after that, followed shortly by another "thump." Apparently, the person with the too-small shoes had thrown both shoes at the wall.

By the time they reached the gallery, they were shaking their heads at the ridiculous comments they heard. If the situation wasn't so tragic, in other circumstances Lily and Carl would have been laughing.

When they reached the princess's bedchambers, there were no royal guards standing sentry duty. The door was wide open. The princess was not in the room. Four servants were diligently cleaning the room. A large woman had picked up the circular rug from the center of the floor and thrown it on the bed. Two women were on their knees scrubbing the floor. The fourth woman was cleaning the huge fireplace.

Carl whispered to Lily, "Where is the princess?"

"Where is the princess? When will she return to her bedchambers?" inquired Lily of the woman working on the rug.

"She is with the seamstresses being fitted for her wedding finery and should return after we finish cleaning her chambers," was the reply.

"Well then, we better get to work now, Will," said Lily.

Carl unhooked the curtains and pulled down the drapes. He placed them on the black settee by the fireplace. When the women finished scrubbing the stone floors and the fireplace was clean and fresh wood placed on the grate, he laid the circular rug back in the center of the room.

Lily had stripped the bed and tucked fresh, clean sheets, and quilts, all black, of course, onto the straw-filled mattress. Until the princess married the baron, she only merited a straw mattress. After their nuptials, she would be given a feather-filled mattress.

Two women carried the curtains and drapes, freshly cleaned, and handed them to Carl. He laid them down on the black settee, again, and set about to rehang them in front of the window.

The four women had completed their work and slipped out of the room, leaving Lily and Carl to finish up their chores.

Carl struggled to put the cleaned duster on top of the oversized four-poster bed, but he managed to finish it with Lily's help.

The only task left to complete was the lowering of the chandelier and refilling it with fresh candles. It was getting dark, and time was running out. Carl was working as slowly as he could so he would still be there when the princess returned to the room.

Lily stood in the doorway and surveyed the entire room. Everything was clean and in order and awaited the princess's arrival back. There was nothing else to do.

"Will, it is time to leave. You have done well. Thank you," said Lily.

As Carl and Lily were closing the door behind them, Princess Charlotte, accompanied by two royal guards, was walking into view from the direction of the gallery. She was wearing a drab-looking dark gray dress with long sleeves and devoid of any lace trim; but no matter what she wore, the princess was still a vision of beauty.

"We just finished cleaning your room, Your Royal Highness," said Carl with a slight bow toward the princess.

"Out of the way!" demanded one of the royal guards pushing Carl aside. They escorted her into the room. Just before they closed the door, the princess turned and gave a small smile to Carl standing in the hallway. She then looked down at her clenched right hand. Carl knew that she was holding his locket and had faith that he would rescue her. He couldn't let her down. He had to get her away from here and before the nuptials the baron scheduled for this evening.

Since Carl had liberated the key to the room last night, the guard had to resort to pulling out a large key ring and sorting through at least fifteen keys to find the right key to the room. He locked the door and placed the key ring on a hook in the wall behind him. He then took his place outside the door on the left. The other royal guard was already on the right side opposite, standing at attention.

Princess Charlotte was so despondent when the door was closed and hearing the key turning in the lock that she walked to the window, pulled the curtains and drapes aside, and gazed out into the darkness. She put her left hand on the stone windowsill, her right hand still clenching Carl's locket. Her fingers felt something different. There were scratches on the sill. Curious, she walked to the chest of drawers, opened the second drawer, and pulled out a candle and candle holder. She lit the candle from the newly started fire in the fireplace, placed it in a holder, and strode back to the window. She placed the candle holder on the sill. Lightly etched in the stone windowsill was, "Have faith, milady. Carl."

She was so absorbed in reading the message that the princess didn't hear the key turning in the lock. Hearing boot steps on the floor, she abruptly turned around and saw the baron standing in the doorway with a servant girl standing behind him. She was holding the white gown the princess was to wear for the wedding.

The baron had been smiling when he first entered the chambers, but he quickly replaced it with a scowl. Something was not right. He asked her what she was so intent upon when he entered the room.

The princess didn't reply. She quickly put her right hand into her pocket and dropped the locket into it.

The baron crossed the room, pushed the princess aside, and looked out the window. Seeing nothing out of the ordinary, he then glanced down at the stone windowsill. From the glow of the candle the princess had brought to the sill, he read the message. He whipped his head around and accusingly said, "Who is Carl?"

The princess replied evenly with her head held high, "I do not know, my lord."

Clearly, the baron did not believe her.

CHAPTER 23

Carl and Lily walked quickly back to the courtyard, where Carl told Lily that he had to return to the stables and do his chores. First, he picked up Billy, carried him back upstairs to his home, and gently laid him on his straw mat.

"We finished stringing the pennants. It took hours, but they are finished. No one was really very happy. Usually everyone likes a celebration and looks forward to a big party, but no one seemed happy today," said Billy.

"You worked hard this afternoon, Billy," said Carl.

"We were told that we all must get dressed in our best clothes and come down to the courtyard in two hours," Billy said while nodding off to sleep.

Carl placed a blanket on Billy and said goodbye to Lily. While climbing down the stairway, he ran into Jake on his way up.

"We worked so hard today that I am very tired. I don't want to go to the party tonight. I hope my mother won't make me," said Jake to Carl. "Will, can you speak to her and ask her to let me stay at home tonight?" he asked.

"Jake, I suggest that you just tell your mother that both you and Billy have both worked harder today than ever before and that you want to go to sleep early. Maybe she will let you stay in bed instead," advised Carl.

Lily had walked out the door to the top of the stairs to look for Jake. She heard their conversation and said, "Billy is sound asleep, and, Jake, you do look very tired. Will is right. You both worked hard today and have earned the right to rest," she stated.

"I have no choice. I have been ordered to attend the festivities. In fact, all of Grimalka have been ordered to partake of the festivities. On the other hand, two small children certainly will not be missed," said Lily.

Jake gave Will a big hug and ran up the stairs, quickly hugging his mother and ran into his home.

90

"This is such a sad day, Will," said Lily.

"I agree," was his reply.

Carl turned and continued his walk down the stairs and went straight to the kitchens.

Upon seeing Larry, hard at work peeling potatoes, Carl pushed through the food preparers in his direction. It was pure pandemonium in the kitchens this evening. There were almost too many people working on the dinner. Larry felt the same way as when he reached Carl's side, he said, "There are so many extra people working this evening, the three of us will never be missed. Besides, we can hardly move around in here."

As Larry and Carl passed by Paul, he immediately put down the bread he was kneading and joined them in walking toward the back door. Rodney had already looked up and seen them coming in his direction. He opened the door just as they got there. The four of them rushed out and closed the door before anyone saw them leave. They raced across the courtyard, grabbed several torches, lit them from the lanterns on the wall, and opened the door to the tunnel.

Upon reaching the other side, they looked around and saw that no one was in sight. Apparently, the stable hands were commandeered to work in the kitchens or perform other duties in preparation for the upcoming wedding.

"Just in case anyone is left behind, let's walk to the hen house. No one ever goes there at this time of day," said Carl. He knew that many villagers worked in the gardens at least three times a week but always returned to the castle shortly after lunch time to perform other duties.

Now that the wedding has been planned for this evening, all their plans for rescuing the princess had to be put aside and new ones devised and quickly.

"There are only four of us and hundreds of them," said Paul despondently.

"We can't just rush into the great dining hall and grab the princess in front of everyone. Our only chance is to get to her before they take her to the hall," said Larry.

"We have less than two hours to formulate our plan and act on it," said Rodney.

After deliberating for fifteen minutes, they could not find a clear way to rescue the princess. The only path open to them was to saddle up the horses as they had planned and then brazenly walk to the princess's room, disable the royal guards at her door, and bring her to the drawbridge. Unfortunately, possibly fifty people could be milling about the upper hallways in preparation for this evening's nuptials.

While they were discussing this last obstacle, Hans came running from the tunnel into the stable yard.

"If you are here, Carl, come quickly," Hans yelled, clearly almost out of breath while looking all around.

"The baron is searching the entire castle for someone called Carl, and he is very angry," shouted Hans.

The men rushed to Hans who was standing in the stables, looking in all directions to find Carl.

"What is going on, Hans?" asked Larry.

"I don't know anything except the baron is now personally going through the villager's homes and will shortly come here too. He said he is putting off the nuptials until Carl is found and executed. And anyone harboring him will be thrown in prison, and I don't want to go to prison!" said Hans excitedly.

"Clearly I must leave here now. Just say that you have not seen me," said Carl as he rushed toward the tunnel.

"Where are you going?" asked Larry as Carl ran past him.

Carl stopped, turned, and said, "To make sure Jake, Billy, and Lily are not thrown in prison." Then Carl grabbed the lit torch Hans just used in the tunnel. He took off running as fast as he could.

By the time Carl reached the courtyard, the baron was halfway up the staircase to Lily's home along with four of his royal guards. Carl rushed to the stairs and managed to reach the doorway as the baron entered Lily's home. The royal guards blocked Carl from entering.

"Where is Carl?" demanded the baron. He was looking directly at Lily.

"I don't know anyone named Carl," replied Lily simply.

"You brought a man with you when you cleaned the princess's bedchambers. Where is he?"

"Directly behind you," said Carl while pushing the royal guards aside.

While the guards started to block Carl from crossing the door threshold, the baron commanded of his royal guards, "Let him enter!"

"Are you Carl?" demanded the baron.

Before Carl could answer they heard, "No, he isn't," stated loudly by Jake.

"He is Will," added Billy.

"Yes, my lord, that is not Carl, but he is Will," said Lily.

"I am Will," Carl said looking the baron right in the eye. "Leave these people alone."

"You are only saying that you are Will to protect this woman and her children," the baron gruffly said.

"Guards, take this man along with the woman and her children to the prisons," bellowed the baron.

Two of the royal guards grabbed Carl, one on each side, and pulled him from the room. One of the other guards picked up Billy as Jake had hurriedly called out that Billy could not walk. The fourth guard roughly put one hand on Lily's arm and grasped Jake's hand in his other hand pushing Lily in front of him and dragging Jake behind him.

Villagers had gathered in the courtyard to see what was happening to Lily and her sweet boys.

"Where are you taking Will?" asked one of the children.

The baron immediately walked over to the child and asked, "What is this man's name? And tell me the truth."

"Will," he replied.

"He is called Will," called out another child.

"Will plays hoops with us," added a small boy walking toward the baron.

Frederick, the burly mustached and bearded cook in charge of the kitchen, had joined the villagers in the courtyard. He pushed forward through the crowd. "He is Will," said Frederick. "He has been in my kitchens. I have heard that little boy," he said pointing at Jake, "and one of the laborers in the kitchen both call him Will."

Realizing he had not found Carl after all, the baron instructed his guards to release Carl, Lily, and her boys.

Carl took Billy from the guard's arms and carried him back upstairs and gently laid Billy on his straw mat.

Jake ran in behind him, closely followed by Lily.

"I am sorry that you were so roughly treated by the baron," said Carl to Lily and the boys.

"Will, can I talk to you outside for a minute?" asked Lily.

Carl followed Lily out the door, closed it and asked Lily what she wanted.

"There were only six of us cleaning the princess's room. You were the last one near the windows, putting up the curtains and drapes. Did you see the message on the sill from Carl that everyone is talking about, Will?" asked Lily.

Carl decided that to keep Lily in the dark for now was safer for her and her family. He would definitely tell her the truth after the princess was safe.

"I did not look at the sill. I only rehung the drapes," replied Carl. "Besides, I am Will, not Carl," he added.

"Thank goodness. I feel so relieved," said Lily with a sigh.

Carl told Lily that he had chores to do at the stables and would see her and the boys later.

CHAPTER 24

Carl slowly made his way through the kitchen. When he got out the back door, he walked hurriedly to the tunnel and through it to the stables. As he emerged from the tunnel, he was immediately greeted by Larry who said, "The horses are saddled. Hans is going to help us. He and Andrew will bring the horses to the courtyard."

Andrew was Hans' assistant and was a quiet boy and a good worker too. He was fair-haired, blue eyed, and four inches taller than Hans, nearly six feet tall. Andrew was as muscular as Hans, and he, also, seemed far too young for such an important job as he was only nineteen. Both Hans and Andrew seemed to have been well educated for simple laborers.

"I don't like the baron and want to help the princess escape before the baron marries her," said Andrew.

Carl hadn't heard Andrew say more than two words together before this. He knew that Andrew really meant what he said.

Larry, Rodney, and Paul had already redeemed their swords from where they were hidden behind the large boulders in the courtyard and placed them in their scabbards that hung from their belts. They were ready for action. As Paul handed Carl his sword, Carl nodded thanks to him and said, "Give me a moment to put on my sword, and we can go save Princess Charlotte."

He turned toward the stable hands and said, "Thank you, Hans and Andrew. We can't release the princess from the baron's clutches without your assistance."

The four men walked purposely through the tunnel and opened the door to the kitchen. Heads turned in their direction as they marched through the kitchen with their swords hanging from their sides and stern looks on their faces.

"Someone has to save the princess from the baron," announced Larry. The men and women looked at each other, and when they realized what the four were going to do, they all started smiling.

One of the kitchen staff called out to the villagers outside the door, "Make room. Princess Charlotte is going to be saved," as the men strode out of the kitchen into the courtyard. Cheers rang out, and the villagers moved away to let them pass.

They ran up the stairs to the upper hallway and walked briskly down the hall pushing aside the men and women they encountered along the way. As they rounded the gallery to gain access to the royal bedchamber area, they heard someone from behind them calling down to people below that "there might be trouble up here."

As soon as the two royal guards at the door to the princess's bedchambers saw them coming, they immediately drew their swords from their scabbards and took a fighting stance.

While rushing around the gallery, Larry, Rodney, Paul, and Carl all pulled their swords from their scabbards and grasped their hilts with firm grips. Larry and Rodney got to the royal guards first and started fighting them immediately. In five strokes, Larry disarmed the guard. He kicked the guard's sword back toward Paul for him to pick up. Rodney was fighting a more skilled swordsman. It took him several minutes longer for the guard to surrender. Both Rodney and the guard received a small cut before Rodney finally won. Paul immediately picked up this second guard's sword.

As the swordplay was ensuing outside the room, Carl put his sword back in his scabbard and then took the key from his pocket, unlocked the door, and rushed in saying to the princess, "Quick. Take my hand. We are leaving now."

The princess had been at the window, looking down at the message Carl had etched in the sill. She didn't hesitate for one second and took hold of Carl's hand, and they left the room. Larry pushed both royal guards into the room and closed the door. He turned the key and locked the door, removing the key and taking it with him.

The men had a quick choice to make. The hallway to the right was filling with the baron's royal guards. The hallway to the left, leading to the gallery was full of men and women dressed in their formal garb for the nuptials. They didn't think twice and headed toward the gallery.

"Look, the princess is with them," said one of the men. They were so upset with the goings on that they didn't know whether to back away from the armed men or curtsy to the princess. The men and women finally moved back against the walls and made room for them to pass, not wanting to be attacked by the drawn swords.

When they neared the end of the hallway by the stairs to the courtyard, several royal guards reached the landing and were headed their way. Paul quickly handed the two guards' swords to Carl and he, Larry, and Rodney began to fight the guards. There were two royal guards to each man. The entire time they were fighting with their swords, the royal guards from the other hallway past the gallery were getting closer to them.

Larry was doing a good job keeping two royal guards at bay at the same time. His swordsmanship was excellent. Larry wounded one and then concentrated on disarming the second guard. Even though Rodney had been injured battling the guard outside the princess's chambers, he was more than holding his own battling two guards at once. He thrust forward one more time, and the royal guard on his right fell down. Turning quickly to his left, he brought his sword around in an arc, waist high, and as his sword hit the royal guard, injuring him, the momentum of the weapon continued around releasing the injured guard's grip on his sword and sending the sword flying down the hall.

Just as Carl looked at him, Paul had knocked down his first opponent. The second royal guard was a pretty good swordsman, and Paul seemed to delight in the challenge.

Carl was shielding the princess from these sword fights as they slowly inched forward, their backs against the wall, toward the court-yard stairs. At one point, Carl handed two of the royal guards' fallen swords to the princess, drew his own sword, and battled a guard. The guard had already been wounded by Larry, so it did not take long for Carl to disarm him. One quick swing followed by a long thrust, and the guard was disarmed and down. Carl then placed his sword back into his scabbard. As he picked up two more of the guards' swords, Carl called to the princess to follow him quickly and run down the stairs.

By the time they reached the courtyard, more royal guards were entering from the direction of the drawbridge. There was only one way to go and that was to the kitchen. He threw the guards' swords he had collected onto the ground and told the princess to drop the swords she was holding and grab his hand. He pulled her into the kitchen and together they worked their way to the back door. The cooks tried to get out of their path as quickly as they could.

Hand in hand, they ran to the tunnel. Carl quickly picked up and lit a torch. Thankfully, the tunnel door was open. When they reached the other end of the tunnel, Carl immediately saw Andrew. By all accounts, Hans and Andrew should have been waiting by the drawbridge with the horses by now.

"Andrew, why are you still here?" queried Carl.

"The baron and two of his royal guards came through the tunnel just as we were about to enter it. He demanded to know where Carl was, and when he saw the saddled horses, he got angrier and said he hadn't ordered any," said Andrew. The saddled horses were now tethered to the fence outside the stables.

"His guards grabbed Hans, bound him with ropes, and threw him into one of the horse stalls. They are all in the stable now. I am supposed to be on the lookout for you. The baron threatened to have Hans killed if I didn't help him," Andrew further said while giving a quick bow to the princess. He hadn't noticed her at first, and now he became flustered.

"As you can see, we have had to have a change of plans," said Carl.

Suddenly, Larry, Paul, and Rodney came running through the tunnel.

Larry closed the tunnel doors and said, "Quick! Help us move a boulder to block the doors."

The five of them pushed and pushed until the large boulder near the entrance finally moved. They managed to block the doors just as they heard yells from inside the tunnel.

"That should keep the guards away for a while as we figure out where to go from here," said Larry.

"They probably won't attempt to reach us by going through Near-Dead Swamp, so we are safe for now," said Paul.

"We have a slight problem, Larry," said Carl. He relayed the information Andrew had just shared with him.

Andrew told them that Hans was held captive in the third stall on the left and that the baron and the guards were in the stall with him, trying to find out as much as they could about Carl.

"We can easily take out two guards and the baron," put in Rodney. And they proceeded to do just that.

Apparently, the baron was not aware that they had released the princess from his grasp because when the royal guards at the stall were overtaken by Larry and Paul, the baron noticed the princess standing in the doorway of the stables. He was angry already, but he turned absolutely livid now. His scowl grew even larger, and he clenched his hands. Even his mustache seemed to stiffen.

Rodney immediately released Hans, and then Hans and Rodney tied up the two guards and left them in the stall. They handed the guards' swords to Carl.

"Rodney, we should arm Hans and Andrew with these swords in case some other situation arises," said Carl as he gave one sword to each of them.

The baron was unarmed since he had his royal guards do all his dirty work. Paul tied the baron's hands together and shoved him into the stall with the guards and closed the stall door. "Release me now, or I'll summon Dreaddrick," ordered the baron.

CHAPTER 25

The six men and the princess had decided to go to the gardens by the hen house and get some vegetables to eat while discussing what action to take next. None of them had eaten with all that was happening so quickly. Andrew pulled up some carrots and radishes while Paul grabbed some beans from the plants. They passed around these harvested vegetables to the others.

"Dreaddrick can be a major problem," said Hans.

"We fully understand that, Hans. We crossed paths with him in the Black Forest," said Larry.

While the men were talking, the princess insisted on tending to the cut Rodney received while fighting the guard outside her chambers. It wasn't deep, but she would not hear of any denials of her cleaning it from Rodney. She washed the blood off his arm and tied a strip of cloth around his arm. She had torn the cloth from her petticoat. The princess felt that it was the least she could do. Rodney didn't like the fuss but secretly enjoyed the fact that a royal princess actually was taking care of his wound.

"In case we have to confront Dreaddrick, what are his weak spots, if any?" asked Larry.

"He doesn't seem to have a weakness that I know of," said Andrew.

"I think he does," said Carl.

They all looked at him in wonder as he had never even heard of Dreaddrick before the princess was kidnapped.

"Dreaddrick's power is weaker in daylight than in darkness," said Carl.

"How would you know that?" asked Rodney.

Carl related his theory to the men. "Jake told me the story of how his brother became lame and his father was killed by Dreaddrick. The wizard was aiming his wand at the fleeing horse and hit and killed Jake's father instead. It was in broad daylight here at the stables. His aim was off. Also, Frankie told us that when Dreaddrick captured him and Silver, it took *two* tries to lasso Silver on two separate occasions. That was in Alauria that is filled with beautiful sunny light. Therefore, I believe that he cannot function as well in daylight as he can in the dark. On the other hand, he had no trouble with keeping Frankie captive and blocking us in the dark depths of the Black Forest."

The men all agreed that what Carl related seemed logical to them. Now they had to figure a way to make that information useful to them in case Dreaddrick appeared.

"I haven't really thought about the old wizard in a long time," said Hans. He sat back and seemed lost in deep thought for a few minutes. Then he said, "When I was really small, there were stories told around the fire at night, something about the wizard losing his spell book."

"I heard about that," jumped in Andrew.

"Do you know any details, Andrew?" asked Carl.

"Yes. Now it is all coming back to me. This is how Baron Nelson gets Dreaddrick to do all his dirty deeds. The baron saw Dreaddrick using the spell book one night, and he watched where the wizard hid it away. While Dreaddrick was off doing something, the baron crept into Dreaddrick's home and stole the book. He then hid it where Dreaddrick couldn't find it, and he won't give it back to him."

"If we could find the spell book, maybe we could make a deal with Dreaddrick," chimed in Princess Charlotte. Up until now she hadn't said a word.

"All we have to do is politely ask the baron to tell us where he hid it, and he will gladly tell us, I suppose," said Hans sarcastically with a frown.

"No, Hans. The princess has a good point. We must figure out a way to make the baron tell us where it is," said Carl.

"What do we have that the baron wants, besides the princess I mean?" asked Larry.

"By marrying the princess, he thought he would become ruler over all of Alauria," said Paul.

"Never!" said both Carl and the princess at the same time.

"But if we let the baron believe that he can marry the princess *after* we retrieve the spell book, maybe that would work," said Larry.

"Of course, we would not let that ever happen. We just want the baron to believe it is possible," said Rodney.

"Before we say another word on that subject, let us try to figure out where he could have hidden the book," said Carl.

"If the great Wizard Dreaddrick couldn't find it, how could we, mere mortals, accomplish that?" asked Paul.

They talked it out for a while, all agreeing that the baron would have hidden the spell book someplace in Castle Grimalka where he could keep an eye on it on a daily basis but also where Dreaddrick couldn't find it. The wizard would have searched all the logical places, so they had to come up with a completely safe but still illogical hiding place.

They had another problem. Even if they could figure out where the spell book was hidden, they couldn't redeem it with all the royal guards after them.

For now, they were safe from the guards, and Dreaddrick had not shown his face yet, so they decided to get some sleep and get a fresh outlook in the morning. They would sleep in shifts with two men standing watch all night while a third kept an eye on their prisoners in the stall.

CHAPTER 26

When it was Carl's and Hans' turn to stand watch, they decided to talk to each other to make sure they stayed awake. Carl had a lot of questions, and hopefully, Hans could supply answers to some of them.

"When did Baron Nelson acquire Castle Grimalka?" asked Carl.

"I heard that it was about the same time as when he stole the wizard's spell book," replied Hans.

"In fact, before the baron stole the book, everyone said he was not as evil as he is now. The power that the spell book gave him over the wizard is what changed him. The Black Forest was not what it is now. It was lush and green and had all sorts of happy animals living in it. There were deer, rabbits, raccoons, squirrels, and many, many birds tweeting merrily. The black clouds were not hovering over the forest. The sun's golden rays filtered broadly through the leaves of the trees. A clear brook ran right down the center of the woods. There were oak trees, maples, hickory, sycamore, and lots of others, in all shades of green as well as brightly colored woodland flowers. I've heard that a magical unicorn used to live in the forest too," explained Hans.

"It is hard to believe that anything beautiful was where Black Forest is now. It is so depressing," said Carl.

"I was told that the Near-Dead Swamp didn't exist as it is today. It was still a swamp, but instead of quicksand, it was filled with cypress trees and lots of wildlife. Turtles would sun themselves on stones. Lily plants bloomed with bright white flowers. There was a creek that meandered through the swamp with water that was calm and clear. All the swamp water was clear also," said Hans. He looked so sad and was shaking his head from side to side as he related his story.

"The moat around the castle had beautiful goldfish shimmering in the sunlight as they swam around," said Hans. "There were colorful flowers bordering the moat. Beautiful white swans also glided across the clear water. There were no electric eels and no quicksand either," he added.

"It all sounds wonderful and magical, Hans. Tell me about the castle itself," urged Carl.

"I did not hear as much about the castle as the lands around it. I will tell you what I do remember. In fact, the more I talk to you, the more stories I recall," said Hans.

"Since all these changes occurred about the time the baron stole the spell book from Dreaddrick, I guess it stands to reason that the baron had the wizard cast a spell over the entire castle grounds to protect the hidden book," suggested Carl.

"That could be right," answered Hans.

Andrew had woken up and joined Carl and Hans. He said, "It is my turn to take watch in a little while. I heard you talking and thought I would relieve one of you."

"I'm not sleepy," said Carl. "You go rest awhile, Hans. Maybe Andrew can fill me in about the castle."

Hans thanked Andrew and told Carl that he hoped he helped him as he lay down where Andrew had been sleeping.

"I only heard a few stories about the castle when I was very little," said Andrew.

"It may help us in our quest for the spell book. Tell me all you know," pleaded Carl.

"My uncle said the castle originally had a drawbridge that was almost always left open. The castle was a friendly place, and everyone was welcome. It was called Gladstone Castle back then, not Castle Grimalka. The inner courtyard had several fountains and many pretty statues with an array of colorful flowers all around them," Andrew began. He looked as sad as Hans did while relating his tale.

"The outside walls were free of all thorny bushes. The castle stood proud and was really very nice looking. The turrets had brightly colored flags waving from them. My uncle used to live in the villager courtyard. There was a huge fountain in the center with brightly colored flowers surrounding it. Even the courtyard in the back by the kitchens was pretty and well landscaped back then," said Andrew.

"What do you know about the gray flag with the black rose in the center that is throughout the castle?" queried Carl.

"The baron added that when he moved in. Before that, I heard that the crest was a field of white with one red rose in the center," said Andrew. "In fact, the baron had the crest in the great dining hall laid twice as he was not happy with the first stone mason's work. The baron, himself, took the stones out after the first installation and stood there and instructed the mason on laying each block the second time. I know that is true as my uncle Douglas was the stone mason, and he is the finest mason in the realm."

"Where is your uncle now, Andrew?" asked Carl.

"He got too old to do masonry as it is hard work and requires lots of heavy lifting. He now lives in King Stephen's castle in Alauria. I miss him," said Andrew sadly.

Carl posed the same question to Andrew that he had asked Hans, "These changes to the castle were about the same time the baron stole the spell book from Dreaddrick. Could the baron have had the wizard cast a spell over the castle to protect the hidden book?"

Andrew replied, "It is really quite possible."

Carl was relieved by Paul, and he went to sleep with a smile on his face. Hans and Andrew had helped him more than they knew.

CHAPTER 27

The next morning, Carl was very excited and could hardly wait for everyone to wake up. After checking on the baron and the guards, Carl asked Hans to take the first morning watch over them. They were going to hold a meeting away from the stable area so the baron would not hear. Carl assured Hans that he would fill him in on everything they discussed.

After the entire group sat down on the small grassy area by the hen house, Carl said he discovered something important while on guard duty. "I think I know where the baron hid Dreaddrick's spell book! The big hurdle will be how to redeem it!"

"Where?"

"How?"

These were the questions every one of his friends asked at the same time.

"Last night, both Andrew and Hans relayed to me all the stories they were told about the castle and the grounds," stated Carl. "I will give you a quick overview of my findings, and then tell you where the spell book is hidden."

Carl was so excited he couldn't sit still while talking. He had to get up and walk around.

"First, Castle Grimalka and the surrounding lands are not what they once were. The Black Forest and the Near-Dead Swamp were both beautiful forests. The moat was not filled with quicksand and electric eels. It was pristine and filled with goldfish, and there were many swans. The castle was called Gladstone Castle and was picturesque with its beautiful statues and flowing fountains. The gray flag and black rose was not the emblem of the castle, but instead it was a single red rose on a white background. The baron must have had Dreaddrick cast a spell on everything, both the castle and the surrounding grounds," he continued.

"Wow," was all Paul could say. The others just sat there, stunned.

"Now what is the location of Dreaddrick's spell book?" asked Larry.

"That was the easy part. Andrew told me exactly where it is, and he still doesn't even know he told me," said Carl.

"Where is it? Tell us now, please!" begged the princess.

"Yes, please," asked Andrew, trying to figure out what he told Carl to lead him to the hiding place of the wizard's spell book.

Carl was enjoying the telling of this tale, but he knew he didn't have time to draw it all out slowly. So he simply said, "The spell book is buried in the stone floor under the emblem of the black rose in the great dining hall."

Carl quickly explained what Andrew told him about his Uncle Douglas. Every one of them agreed that that had to be the baron's hiding place. He would be in the great dining hall every day so he could tell if anyone discovered his secret cache and dug up the floor.

"We have almost no chance of getting out of here without a major battle with the baron's royal guards. How can we possibly gain access to the great dining hall *and* dig it up?" queried Larry.

In fact, while they were having this discussion, loud noises were heard coming from the direction of the tunnel. Apparently, the guards were using a battering ram to force the doors open. It was only a matter of time before they could figure out a way to break through.

CHAPTER 28

They decided to try and recover the spell book as quickly as possible. In order to do that, they had to get past the royal guards in the tunnel first. Hans and Andrew figured that there were only about fifty guards in Baron Nelson's army at the most. They determined that they had already wounded ten yesterday, and two more guards were tied up in the stable stall. That left thirty-eight royal guards between them and freedom and the spell book. The six of them could not take on six or seven guards each at one time. They had to lessen the number of guards or find more weapons to take out several guards at a time.

Carl mused that he made a slingshot in order to get a beehive down from a tall tree in the woods back home. "What if we build a much larger one, like a catapult?" His idea was welcomed by all.

Hans and Andrew set off to gather large stones and put them in a pile about twenty feet in front of the doors to the tunnel. Paul and Rodney went about to gather wood to make the platform for the catapult. Larry and Carl were planning the best design for their machine.

Princess Charlotte did not know what they were talking about.

Carl explained, "It is really simple. First, we will take a bucket from the stables and cut it down to the shape of a large bowl. Ropes would be tied to the base. These ropes will hold back our improvised bucket. The whole thing will sit on four pieces of wood tied together in a square shape and be the base for the catapult. We will weigh down the catapult frame with heavy rocks for stability. All we have to do is load rocks into the bowl, pull back the ropes and then release them. The large stones in the bowl will become hard projectiles and take out the guards when the mechanism is released."

In actuality, the construction of the catapult was more intricate, but the princess only needed to know the basics.

The plan was to roll the boulder away from only one of the tunnel doors. As the royal guards came through, Hans and Andrew would set off the catapult, hitting the guards. The guards that were not taken out by the catapult would be "introduced" to Larry, Rodney, Paul, and Carl's swords.

"I can continue to gather large stones for Hans and Andrew," said Princess Charlotte.

"No! You will be safely hidden in the stables in case any guards get past us. We will not have it any other way!" stated Carl firmly.

It took the men only about half an hour to put their catapult together. They took a few practice shots and then declared it ready for action.

The princess was unhappy that she would not be allowed to participate, but she acquiesced and waited by the stall where the baron and the royal guards were being held captive. The least she could do was keep an eye on them.

As she was walking to the stall, Paul and Rodney were struggling to push the boulder away from the tunnel doors. They only pushed it far enough for one door to open, leaving the second one wedged closed. They quickly pulled their swords from their scabbards and stood on one side of the door. Larry and Carl were already standing at the other side in case any guards came through before Paul and Rodney finished moving the boulder.

Two royal guards rushed out the open door. Larry yelled, "Fire!" to Hans and Andrew. The first few stones hit right on target, as they had during their practice session a short time ago. The two guards immediately fell down, badly injured.

Then three royal guards came running out, swords raised, only to trip over the two fallen guards. Carl immediately took the five swords and threw them in a pile off to the side as Larry took care of the guards.

They continued to eliminate the royal guards in this same fashion until the pile of guards almost blocked the door completely.

In less than fifteen minutes, Hans counted the swords and then said there should only be three more royal guards. The men easily finished off the rest of the guards. They then loaded all the swords onto one of the kitchen carts.

Paul and Hans agreed to stay back and stand watch over the baron and his prisoners and to protect the princess. Carl, Larry, Rodney, and Andrew were going to try to dig up the spell book.

When they reached the kitchen side of the tunnel, the door was closed and appeared to be locked. Try as they might, they could not budge the door.

"We warned you to stop that," was yelled from the other side of the door. "We will not let you out!"

"That sounds like Frederick," said Larry.

Larry banged on the door again and said loudly, "Frederick, this is Larry. Please let us out."

"How do we know it is really Larry?" queried Frederick.

"I am the best potato peeler you have ever had in your kitchens," replied Larry.

Immediately they heard the key opening the lock and shortly thereafter the door was flung open.

"We knew you were in trouble when we saw the royal guards all chasing after you, but we have very few weapons other than my kitchen knives," said Frederick.

Carl could see that most of the villagers were standing behind Frederick. The courtyard was packed.

"What happened to all the guards?" asked one of the men.

"We took care of them all. As for weapons, we have a kitchen cart full of swords if you need any," said Larry as Rodney and Carl pulled the cart out of the tunnel door.

"We have something important to attend do," said Carl as the three of them headed in the direction of the kitchens. The crowd cleared a path for them, patting them on their backs as they passed. Carl stopped just outside the kitchen doorway and asked, "Do any of you have pick axes or shovels?"

"We sure do, sir," replied one of the villagers. "Come with me, and I'll get them for you," he added.

The four of them literally ran through the kitchen into the courtyard. The man motioned for them to follow him to an alcove in the wall. Propped against the wall were a dozen shovels and two pick axes. Carl and Larry each grabbed a shovel while Rodney and Andrew each picked up a pick axe. They turned and ran through the courtyard and over to the doorway by the drawbridge. The main entrance to the great dining hall stood in front of them.

CHAPTER 29

Taking a deep breath, Carl opened one of the two massive wooden doors and strode to the center of the hall. He stood on the black rose in the center of the design. Larry, Rodney, and Andrew followed closely behind him.

"Where do we begin, Carl?" asked Andrew.

"Right in the exact center of the design on the black rose," replied Carl moving aside and stepping off the rose.

Andrew and Rodney each raised their arms with the pick axes gripped tightly in their hands and proceeded to smash them down on the stone floor. After a few tries, the stones started to give a little.

Carl and Larry used the shovels to remove the loosened stones that Andrew and Rodney managed to pry loose.

Several minutes later, "We found it!" called out Andrew. He bent over and pulled out a book that was at least eighteen inches tall, eight inches wide, and four inches thick. The cover was comprised of thick black leather and had nothing inscribed on it.

Andrew handed the book to Carl who flipped open the cover. As he quickly thumbed through some pages, all he could see were squiggles, drawings, and words in a language he did not understand. "This definitely is the wizard's spell book," announced Carl.

The men quickly retraced their steps through the kitchen to the back courtyard. Carl was holding the spell book in his left hand, clutching it to his chest as he ran.

All the villagers were still standing near the entrance to the tunnel. Apparently, a few of the royal guards had regained consciousness and came back through the tunnel because at least nine of them had been subdued and were being held captive. Twenty villagers, armed with the swords, kept the guards at bay in the center of a huge circle of villagers.

Two more guards stumbled out of the tunnel and were immediately pushed to the circle by some villagers and added to the other captives. Rodney volunteered to stay here for a short while to aid the villagers.

Fearing that some royal guards may have gone into the stables where Princess Charlotte was awaiting their return, Carl immediately entered the tunnel and ran through to the other side. He encountered one guard who was quite groggy, but Carl shoved him to the wall with his free right hand and kept running. Larry, who was only about a foot behind Carl, grabbed the guard and passed him back to Andrew saying, "Take him back to the villagers to join his other companions and then hurry back here."

"There should be about two dozen more royal guards by the stable," said Larry. "You continue on to check on the princess, and Andrew and I will stay here and hold the guards down."

In the stable, ten royal guards stood at attention outside the stall. Inside the stall Paul and Hans were lying on the floor, hands and feet bound together with rope. Princess Charlotte was standing, her back against the wall, facing the baron, tears slowly rolling down her cheeks.

Carl stashed the wizard's spell book inside the first stall and then walked toward the guards. He was immediately grabbed by two of the guards and shoved inside the stall.

"I am sorry, Carl," said Hans when Carl was thrown into the stall.

"Aha! Apparently I was correct when I said you were Carl and not Will," the baron angrily said while glaring at Carl.

"But how nice for you to show up in time to hear the latest plans for my nuptials," snarled the baron while staring directly at Carl. He went on to say, "Since you and your two friends here will not be alive to take part in the festivities, you will be delighted to learn all of the details."

While two of his royal guards were binding Carl with ropes, the baron continued his boastful tale. "In a very few moments, Princess Charlotte and I shall depart for her chambers where she will be attended to by her handmaidens. They shall dress the princess in her white silk wedding gown and satin slippers. One of the ladies-in-waiting will comb her glorious blond curls and attach her delicate veil that has a fifteen foot train and has been adorned with tiny black pearls. She shall carry a bouquet of black roses, tied with a white satin ribbon."

The baron was almost dancing while he was relating his nuptials to be. "I will be attended to by my many man servants and shall be clad in a black velvet suit, trimmed in white ermine fur. My black leather dress boots will have been polished to such a shine as to reflect the beautiful princess from across the great hall. Atop my head I shall wear a gold crown studded with many rubies and black pearls. Immediately upon the completion of our betrothal vows I shall rise in stature from Baron Nelson to His Royal Highness, Prince of Alauria. When King Stephen passes on, which incidentally will be very sudden and quite soon, I shall be elevated to the highest title in the entire kingdom. I will be His Majesty the King of Alauria," continued the baron with excitement.

He turned to face the princess and said, "After the ceremony, Princess Charlotte shall have a crown matching mine placed on her head. Of course, her crown will be a much smaller one than mine, but it, too, shall be gold and inlaid with a few rubies and some black pearls." The baron was getting more and more excited as he spun his tale of his upcoming nuptials. He was raising his arms and hands gesturing as he spoke.

The baron continued on, "The wedding shall be witnessed by one hundred of my closest friends in the great dining hall, directly above the black rose design in the stone floor. Then we shall climb the gallery staircase, walk down the hallway to the alcove above the villager's courtyard where we shall be praised and welcomed as His Royal Highness and Her Royal Highness by all my subjects standing below. The courtyard, in addition to the great dining hall, will have been decorated with many streamers and flags. I have even allowed one barrel of my poorest grade wine to be sent to the villagers' courtyard for them to toast the happy couple," bragged the baron while stroking his mustache with his right hand.

"Her Royal Highness and I shall immediately set out for King Stephen's castle in Alauria to officially claim my title and allow the king to introduce *me*, I mean, introduce us at a great celebration open to all the subjects of Alauria. Therefore, upon King Stephen's sudden demise, the people of Alauria will know that I am his successor and their new king." The baron held his head high and grinned.

The entire time Baron Nelson was outlining his soon to be nuptials, tears continued to roll down the princess's cheeks. It hurt Carl to see her so upset. Time was running out for him to stop this tragedy before it occurred.

Suddenly there was a commotion behind Carl. Larry and Andrew were being dragged toward the stall.

"Ah, I see the rest of your men have decided to join you in your final hours. I should say, their final hours too!" bragged Baron Nelson.

"We were jumped from behind as we were taking care of the guards. We should have realized there were more guards loose in the stables as there were only ten left by the tunnel entrance," Larry managed to relate to Carl before the guard holding him picked him up and shoved him into the stall. Then Andrew was pushed in beside him. Four of the royal guards proceeded to secure Larry and Andrew's hands and feet with ropes and then threw them both to the floor. The guards then rolled them over to where Paul and Hans were lying, knocking Hans into the baron in the process.

"I see it is time to *execute* all my plans. Please pardon my little joke, but *execute* is what will happen to you five while I *execute* my wedding plans," boasted the baron.

CHAPTER 30

Meanwhile, a few more royal guard stragglers came through the tunnel into the kitchen courtyard. The villagers quickly added them to their ever-filling circle of captive guards.

"Frederick, it seems that you and the villagers have everything under control here. I better join Carl and Larry now," said Rodney.

He cautiously checked the tunnel, his sword drawn in case more royal guards should enter the tunnel before he reached the stable end. Rodney walked through the tunnel without incident. There should have been close to a dozen guards there, but he didn't see any. When he arrived at the stable entrance, he saw some guards standing outside the third stall and knew it meant trouble.

Rodney crept into the first stall and immediately spied the spell book where Carl had hurriedly stashed it. He picked it up and looked for a place to put the book for safekeeping. Apparently, this stall was not used on a regular basis for horses but rather for storage of tack, feed, and tools for sweeping and mucking out the stables. On one wall, there were hooks holding feed bags and other riding paraphernalia. He put the book inside a bucket that was hooked on the wall and looked around for something to further secrete the hiding place. Rodney found a torn horse blanket and shoved part of it inside the bucket on top of the book, letting the rest of the blanket drape over the sides. It looked like it had been there for quite a while. It was perfect for a temporary hiding place. He put his sword on the floor near the entrance of the stall and pulled straw over it.

As soon as Rodney stuck his head out of the stall, one of the royal guards spotted him and rushed over, his sword drawn. Since the guard could clearly see that Rodney was unarmed, the guard got behind Rodney and roughly pushed him toward the stall where his friends were being held captive.

Just as two of the royal guards were preparing to bind Rodney's hands and feet, a loud *sshump* was heard, and the wizard, Dreaddrick, suddenly appeared in the center of the stall.

"Where have you been?" demanded the baron looking angrily at Dreaddrick. "I have had my hands full with these six men. They tried to kidnap my betrothed and halt the wedding. They have disrupted everything!" said the baron with disgust in his voice.

"I have other things to do besides babysit you, Baron," said Dreaddrick angrily.

"Now, now, keep your temper, Dreaddrick," said Baron Nelson. "Don't forget that I have your spell book. If you ever want it back, you must do as I say!"

"But you don't have the spell book anymore, Baron," said Carl proudly.

Everyone's eyes immediately focused on Carl. The baron's eyes looked angrier than ever. Dreaddrick's looked questioningly. The princess's eyes were hopeful. Larry and Andrew just smiled at Carl. Paul and Hans hadn't yet found out about the liberation of the spell book, so when they looked at Carl, he nodded his head and gave them a small smile. Rodney gave Carl a big wink of his eye and tilted his head ever so slightly in the direction of the first stall. Carl realized that Rodney may have found where Carl stashed the book and done something with it before he arrived moments ago. That was a welcome surprise to Carl.

"Utter nonsense," replied the baron. But still, Carl had given the baron something to think about. Carl looked so smug that the baron was getting a little worried.

Baron Nelson turned and started to walk out of the stall. "Secure the last of their friends," he said, nodding in Rodney's direction. He motioned to four of the royal guards to remain and keep watch over his six captives and signaled for the rest of the guards to accompany him. "Bring the princess with you," he commanded. "We have a wedding to attend."

While standing in the stall doorway, the baron cautiously stated to Dreaddrick, "For the time being, do not execute these men. We will hold a ceremonial hanging after the nuptials for all to see." The baron was also thinking that on the slight chance these men really did find the spell book, he would be able to coerce them into revealing where they were hiding it before their public execution.

CHAPTER 31

By the time the baron and his royal guards reached the other end of the tunnel, the kitchen courtyard was empty. Frederick and the villagers had ushered their captives down to the kitchen cellar and were standing watch over them there. Almost every villager was now armed with a sword. Before Rodney had left them, he advised Frederick to find a secure location to place the guards and instructed them on holding sentry shifts over their captives. The villagers not assigned to watch duty had returned to their homes, along with their newly acquired swords. In case anything untoward happened, Rodney advised them to hide their swords in their homes and then to act as normal as possible. This the villagers happily did.

Rather than walk completely around the castle through the courtyards, the baron and his royal guards, along with Princess Charlotte in tow, decided to take the shortcut through the now almost empty kitchens. Immediately upon seeing Frederick, the baron said, "Get the rest of your kitchen staff back here and prepare the wedding feast. The festivities are on again and will begin shortly."

Frederick did not know what to do or say. When he saw the princess, he could tell that she was being forced to accompany the baron, but there were too many of the royal guards for Frederick and his few kitchen laborers to attempt to stop them.

"Yes, my lord," replied Frederick. "We can have the dinner ready in about one hour, if that pleases you."

"That will give me ample time to properly prepare. Don't be late, and it better be the finest dinner you have ever served," said the baron looking around at the venison, duck, beef, soups, aromatic sauces, various vegetables, and pastries already laid out on the kitchen worktables.

Immediately upon passing through the inner courtyard door, the baron went directly up the staircase to his private quarters after instructing his royal guards to bring the princess directly to her chambers and order the servants to bring her the wedding finery.

The royal guards escorted the princess to her chambers. The guard found the key to her room on the huge key ring that was left hanging on the wall by the previous guards on sentry duty and secured the lock. He took the stance of being the guard outside her chambers.

The second royal guard on duty walked past the princess's door and continued walking down the hall toward the far stairs. He was headed for the seamstress's room to advise her of the baron's latest wishes.

Immediately Princess Charlotte walked across the room to the window and placed her left hand over the message Carl had etched in the stone. It comforted her to know that Sir Lawrence, Sir Rodney, Sir Paul, Carl, and the stable hands tried to rescue her. She was very saddened about their being held captive by the evil baron and the wizard, Dreaddrick. Princess Charlotte put her right hand in her pocket and pulled out the locket Carl had given her while tears started trickling over her cheeks. *"I must have faith,"* she told herself as she wiped the tears away.

The princess heard a key turn in the lock at her door and hurriedly walked to the black velvet settee and sat down as the door opened. She quickly put her right hand into her pocket and secreted the locket. The seamstress and two handmaidens entered the room, the seamstress carrying her wedding gown, and a handmaiden holding her satin slippers. The third had the long bridal veil clutched in her arms.

Two royal guards then entered the room carrying a large wooden tub for the princess to bathe in. They were followed by two villagers with a large water bucket with steam wafting across the top in each of their hands. A handmaiden came in last carrying bathing oils and a towel. The men emptied the four buckets into the tub and left the chambers. The handmaiden poured the oils into the tub and stood aside holding the towel.

The other handmaidens proceeded to undress the princess and help her into the tub.

"Wait," she told the girl carrying her discarded dress toward the door. "Bring the dress back to me. I left my handkerchief in one of the pockets. It was given to me by my sister, and I want to have it during the ceremony," the princess explained.

As the girl started to put her hand into the dress pocket, the princess cried out, "No. Your hands must not touch the handkerchief. It is very special. Hand me the gown."

The girl did as instructed and held the dress out to the princess who put her hand into the pocket and extracted the handkerchief, secreting the locket under it.

The entire time the handmaidens were assisting the princess in her bathing, she held her hand over the edge of the tub so as not to get the handkerchief and locket wet.

The two handmaidens assisted Princess Charlotte out of the tub and dried her off with the towel from the third handmaiden, and then enveloped her in a large coverlet.

The seamstress picked up the wedding dress from the black settee where she had placed it upon entering the room before the princess's bath. She assisted the princess into her underclothing and large petticoat first. Then she and one of the handmaidens helped her put on the wedding gown. There were many small pearl buttons on the back of the dress from the top of the neckline to below her waist. It was a time-consuming task to fasten them all.

Princess Charlotte seated herself on the black settee by the fireplace when her lady-in-waiting entered the chambers to assist in the final preparations. The lady-in-waiting slowly brushed the princess's beautiful long blond tresses until her hair shown a glorious golden color, shimmering in the light of the roaring fireplace.

One of the handmaidens placed the satin shoes on the princess's feet. When she stood, her lady-in-waiting brought the veil with the long train to the princess and fastened it securely in her hair, also attaching it to the back of the shoulders of the gown as it was so long and heavy the hair barrettes could not keep the train in place.

Princess Charlotte was an exquisite vision in the wedding finery. It was a terrible shame that she was to wear it to be wed to the evil Baron Nelson.

CHAPTER 32

While the princess was being dressed by her entourage in her bed-chambers, the baron was being outfitted in his wedding garb by his man servants in his chambers.

He had been bathed and his black velvet suit trimmed in white ermine fur was laid out on his bed. He was about to put his formal clothing on when there was harsh knocking on his bedchamber door. In fact, he had already donned the black velvet pants trimmed with white ermine cuffs. The knocking was loud and persistent. Baron Nelson bellowed to one of the two of his royal guards who were removing his large wooden bathtub from the chambers, "Go to the door and have them stop that infernal racket. I am preparing for my wedding!"

"My lord, you must come at once," exclaimed one of his royal guards who had been knocking on the door.

"You do not order me about! I am in command here!" replied the baron angrily.

"I left word with the sentries at my chamber doors that I was not to be disturbed until I was fully prepared for the wedding!" the agitated baron continued.

"But, my lord, the great dining hall has been vandalized," said the guard.

Quickly Baron Nelson reached for the shirt he had been wearing before his bath. He called for his man servant to bring his boots immediately.

"Which ones, my lord, the daily pair or your formal pair?" meekly asked the servant.

"Either one. I don't care," stated the baron gruffly.

Each man servant grabbed a boot and shoved the boot onto the baron's feet.

Baron Nelson quickly ran from his chambers with four of his royal guards running along closely behind him. As they left the room, the two man servants looked each other in the eye and started to laugh.

"We really shouldn't laugh," said one.

"Yes. We will be in trouble but still…" said the other, muffling laughter.

"When the baron realizes that he is wearing two different boots, his formal one on his right foot and his daily boot on his left foot, he will probably put us in prison," said the first one.

"But the boots match the rest of his outfit. He is wearing his formal black velvet pants trimmed with white ermine fur and his dirty black shirt," said the other man servant. Then they both proceeded to laugh out loud again.

"Let's get out of here quickly!"

They left the baron's bedchambers, giggling all the way down the hall. In fact, both of them were actually happily skipping, not walking.

CHAPTER 33

Baron Nelson was outraged when he saw the condition of the floor in the great dining hall. His face turned beet red. His eyes glared. He was shaking his clenched fists. The royal guards backed away from him fearful for their safety. No one had ever witnessed the baron in such an angry state. He was known for having a quick rise to a temper, but this was unbelievable. This was not the time to mention the baron's clothing, as if anytime would be a good time, all the royal guards mused while stifling smiles.

"I will personally cut off Carl's head!" the baron shouted while running out of the great dining hall.

"But, my lord, the stone masons can repair this in about an hour, and all will be ready for your wedding," ventured one of his royal guards while running after the baron.

The four royal guards kept pace with Baron Nelson as they raced through the courtyard to the kitchens. The baron never noticed the smiles on the villagers' faces when they looked in his direction.

The kitchen was almost immovable as so many people were in the midst of preparing the feast. Baron Nelson and his four royal guards had to slowly weave in and out in order to make their way past the cooks and the food trays and kettles. As he pushed past the workers, they all began to smile. One of them started to laugh out loud, and Frederick quickly clapped his hand over the cook's mouth just in time while stifling a chuckle himself. As soon as the baron and the royal guards exited through the kitchen door, one of the dish-washers grabbed the door handle and quickly shut the door just as a great roar of laughter rang out through the entire kitchen.

The baron and his royal guards rushed to the tunnel entrance and sped through it faster than anyone ever did before. They reached the stable stall in record time where the men were being held captive. The six men were still bound and lying on the floor where the baron had left them. His four royal guards were standing outside the stall. Dreaddrick was talking with the captives.

While Baron Nelson was back at the castle preparing for his nuptials, Carl and his friends were negotiating with Dreaddrick about the spell book. Carl almost had the wizard convinced that he had secured the spell book. He described its size, shape, and what he saw when he flipped through several pages. To make his story more believable, Carl told the wizard where the baron had secreted the book and where he quickly stashed it. But when Dreaddrick sent one of the baron's royal guards to the stall to find it, he could not locate it. They were lucky that Rodney had found it and rehidden it. Carl knew that Rodney did that because of the wink he had given to Carl after they were captured.

Since Carl could describe the spell book in detail, Dreaddrick finally believed that Carl really did find it and that the baron no longer had it in his possession. The wizard was going to give Baron Nelson one try, and only one, at producing the spell book before he took any action. The baron had been ordering the wizard around and not returning the spell book to him for far too long.

Baron Nelson wanted to confront Carl but couldn't admit in front of Dreaddrick that he no longer had the spell book in his possession. Therefore, he had to hide the rage he felt.

"I see you are dressed in your wedding finery," said Paul with a wide grin while looking at the baron.

"You look almost as good as you described to us in vivid detail before you left us," chuckled Larry.

When Dreaddrick burst out laughing, they all lost it and joined in laughing so hard it hurt their sides. They doubled over clutching their stomachs no longer noticing the ropes binding their hands. No one had ever seen Dreaddrick smile, much less execute a hearty laugh. Even the royal guards could hold it back no longer and finally added to the already loud laughter.

CHAPTER 34

The baron was absolutely mortified. How dare everyone laugh at him! He was going to order his royal guards to drag them all into the castle and throw them into the dungeon prison to await public execution, but his own royal guards were laughing at him also.

"Dreaddrick!" yelled the baron so angrily his face was no longer red but now a deep purple. "Stop! Immediately! I command you!"

When they didn't stop laughing, the baron again yelled, "Dreaddrick, make them all stop laughing at me this instant!"

Dreaddrick could laugh no longer. He was drained. He took a deep breath and glared at Baron Nelson. Everyone else finally caught their breaths. The gravity of the situation set back in. One at a time, the royal guards slowly slunk out of the stall and down the stable walkway. All eight of them knew that they were in trouble with the baron and wished to put as much space between them and the baron as they could until he had calmed down, if he ever could calm down. They walked to the tunnel and broke into a run when they entered the tunnel entrance not stopping until they reached the kitchen courtyard.

Frederick had asked two villagers to keep watch at the tunnel entrance after the baron and his royal guards left the kitchens earlier in the evening. He knew there would be trouble because of the scowl on the baron's red face, especially the way the baron was clothed. Frederick had to chuckle every time he remembered what the baron was wearing.

As soon as the villagers heard the royal guards running in the tunnel, they signaled for their fellow villagers to get prepared to capture them. Before the guards reached the courtyard, thirty villagers, armed with swords, were gathered at the tunnel door. They may not have had the special training the royal guards had, but the villagers managed to capture the eight guards and hustle them down the kitchen cellar stairs to join their other captives.

Baron Nelson told Dreaddrick to destroy five of the men, leaving Carl for him to personally take care of.

Dreaddrick looked Baron Nelson in his eyes and said, "Do you still have my spell book in your possession?"

"Of course," said the baron lying. He was not going to let Dreaddrick out of his power. He needed him.

Dreaddrick drew his wand from his pocket, held it up high, and murmured a strange incantation as he lowered his wand straight out directly in front of him. Immediately all the ropes binding Carl, Larry, Rodney, Paul, Hans, and Andrew loosened and fell to the floor. They were released from their bondages, and each one of them slowly stood up and faced Baron Nelson. They no longer laughed at his ridiculous clothing. The gravity of the situation had returned.

"Stop!" ordered the baron. "Don't release them! I order you to bind them back up and throw them into my prison!" The baron was getting red in the face again, completely forgetting how ridiculously he was garbed.

Dreaddrick calmly looked at the baron and said, "I have reason to believe that you may have 'lost' my spell book and that Carl now has it in his possession. But to be fair to both of you, I will give you each one hour in which to return here to me with the book in your hands."

The baron turned his back on them all. He walked out of the stall planning to hide nearby so he could follow Carl. When Carl retrieved Dreaddrick's spell book, the baron would attack him and take back the spell book. The baron would then bring the spell book to the wizard. Or even better, instead of returning it to Dreaddrick, he would again hide the book and thereby regain control of Dreaddrick again. The baron planned on tearing a page out of the spell book and showing it to the wizard as proof of his possession of it. Then he could have the wizard destroy Carl and his cohorts while he watched. For the first time this evening, the baron smiled.

CHAPTER 35

"Dreaddrick," began Carl. "We definitely have your spell book in our possession. We will return your book to you, but we have several conditions before doing so."

"Yes," said Larry.

"We must have your word that you will perform the tasks we ask, or we will destroy the book," said Paul.

Rodney said, "In fact, we would like you to complete these tasks *before* we hand over the spell book."

"Before we give you our list of tasks, we must release the princess from the baron's clutches," said Carl.

"Very well," replied Dreaddrick. "But be back here in one hour with the spell book, or you will all be sorry."

The six men grabbed their swords and hurried from the stables, through the tunnel, and quickly walked into the kitchens.

"Frederick, the nuptials are off again. As you could probably tell by the baron's attitude as he came through here to the main castle, he…"

"But Larry, he never came back through here. The last we saw him, he was dressed in ridiculous clothing and accompanied by four of his royal guards headed toward the stables," interrupted Frederick.

"He must still be in the stable area waiting to attack us when we return with the book," said Paul.

"In case he is following us, he will be unarmed and alone. Please feel free to detain him with his royal guards in your cellar," said Rodney.

Frederick smiled and said, "I will be glad to make sure the baron spends some quality time with his royal guards."

The six men continued on their quest to rescue Princess Charlotte. They hurried up the archway staircase and down the hall toward the gallery. Upon reaching the gallery they each looked over the railing at the empty great dining hall. The black rose could not be seen in the center of the room. The stones were piled as they left them when they unearthed the spell book.

When they reached the princess's bedchamber, there were two royal guards standing sentry outside her door. Larry and Paul walked up to the guards and Paul calmly said, "The baron asked us to talk to the princess."

Looking at their villager garb, one of the guards said, "I think not. Begone!"

Both Larry and Paul put their hands on their sword hilts and quickly unsheathed their swords. The royal guards did the same. Rodney pulled out his sword and joined in on the melee. As the swordplay drew the men away from the door, Carl removed the key to Princess Charlotte's bedchamber from his vest pocket and unlocked the door. Hans and Andrew both pulled out their swords and took the royal guards' places at the sides of the door.

Carl rushed to the princess who was standing at the window, clasping his locket in her right hand and gazing out into the dark night. She was a beautiful vision in her bridal gown, even with the tears running down her cheeks. Carl had never seen such a wonderful sight in his life.

"We have found a way to get out of Castle Grimalka and away from the evil Baron Nelson. Come with us now, Your Royal Highness," said Carl gazing into her beautiful blue eyes.

"Thank goodness," sighed the princess. "You and your locket have been sustaining me through this entire ordeal."

She took the veil from her hair and pulled the train off her shoulders. "There is no time for you to change your dress," warned Carl. "We must leave now."

When they walked through the door and started down the hallway, Andrew and Hans immediately followed them. They walked toward the gallery and then down the other hall toward the courtyard below.

"Sorry we're so late," said Larry as he, Rodney, and Paul caught up with Carl and the princess. "We had a little business to finish," he said nodding back toward the two royal guards now lying on the floor twenty feet behind them.

"Hans, tell Frederick to send some of his villagers to drag these two guards to the kitchen cellars," said Larry.

As they all entered the kitchen, Hans immediately informed Frederick of their request.

"We're almost out of room. Isn't it great?" was Frederick's response to Hans.

"By the way, the baron has not shown his face here," called Frederick after them.

Carl thought it better that the princess not be subjected to anything more at this point, so he told Larry, Rodney, Hans, and Andrew to wait for him at the entrance to the tunnel. Then he and Paul escorted Princess Charlotte to Lily's home.

Carl knocked gently on the door hoping to gain Lily's attention and not wake the boys.

To his surprise, both Lily and Jake answered the door. Carl stepped in and told Lily that he had a special request.

"Anything, Will," Lily replied.

"First of all, I must confess that my real name is Carl," he said. "I apologize for keeping that a secret from you, but as a stranger in Grimalka, I felt it better that no one knew who I was," he continued. "Then it was safer for you and your family to believe I was really Will. Please forgive me," he pleaded to Lily.

"That's okay," Jake immediately responded.

"Of course, I understand," said Lily.

"What is your request, Carl, especially at this late hour?" Lily asked.

"I need to protect someone for the rest of the night, and your home is the safest place I could think of," said Carl.

As Lily agreed by nodding her head and smiling, Carl turned to the door and opened it, motioning for the princess and Paul to come inside.

"Your Royal Highness," said Lily making a quick curtsy as soon as she saw Princess Charlotte. Clearly, Lily was very flustered at seeing the princess walking through the doorway to her simple home.

Jake said, "Wow. A real princess…in our home! And you are so beautiful," said Jake so excitedly that he woke Billy.

"Bow to Her Royal Highness," admonished Lily to Jake. He immediately complied and said, "Billy can't bow. He can't walk." He pointed to his brother lying on the straw mat behind him. "I'm Jake!"

The princess smiled at Jake, said, "Thank you, Jake." She then looked at Lily said, "Thank you, Lily, and you too, Billy," as she walked to Billy, bent over, and held out her hand to him. By the look on everyone's face, the princess instantly had won the hearts of Lily and her family.

"Sir Paul will stand guard outside your door," said Carl nodding toward Paul. "Thank you so very much. I shall return in the morning and collect the princess. We just needed someplace where she could rest for a few hours, out of harm's way."

"You are in good hands, Princess Charlotte," said Carl.

Carl did not know, but as this was the first time he addressed her as Princess Charlotte and not Your Royal Highness, the use of her first name by him made her heart flutter. All he did know was that when he said goodbye to everyone, her smile was all he noticed, and it warmed him tremendously.

CHAPTER 36

"The baron must be waiting for us near the stable," said Larry when Carl joined them. "Everyone keep a sharp look out for him."

Hans lit one torch and walked behind Larry and Carl. Andrew and Rodney followed closely at the back.

"Our hour is up," said Carl as they were walking through the tunnel.

"Yes, and Dreaddrick will be waiting for the baron or us to produce his spell book," said Larry.

Rodney looked at Carl and said, "We probably shouldn't produce the book until we finish our negotiations, right?"

Carl and Larry both agreed.

The stable yard was still well lit with lanterns, but the stable itself was dark. Neither the baron nor the wizard was in sight.

"Let's flush out the baron," whispered Larry to Carl.

"Good idea," said Rodney, motioning for Hans and Andrew to walk on either side of the stable. Rodney quickly walked toward the cow corral and out of sight.

As soon as the three men were in place, Larry said loudly to Carl, "You better fetch the wizard's spell book now, Carl, so we can meet with Dreaddrick. I'll wait here for your return."

Carl replied, "I'm on my way." He then walked off in the direction of the hen house.

Less than a minute after Carl walked away, the baron snuck out of the stable, his back brushing closely to the stable wall. He then quietly rushed to the pigpen fence and ducked to the height of the fence in order to remain hidden. As the courtyard in the stable area was the only place lit by lanterns at this hour of the morning, the baron thought he could not be seen following Carl this far away under the cover of darkness.

Hiding in the dark can work two ways. If the baron could not be easily seen, neither could Rodney, Hans, or Andrew. All three met together behind the baron. The baron was so intent in watching and following Carl so he could jump him and steal the spell book that he didn't know what was happening behind him. The three men stood looking down at the baron crouched by the fence, and Rodney said, loudly, "Ahem."

"Look what strange creatures sneak around here late at night," said Hans.

"We should set out some large rat traps," added Andrew.

Baron Nelson was so startled that he fell backward, landing on his back side right into a huge pile of manure.

Hans and Andrew bent over, and each grabbed one of the baron's arms and pulled him upright. Rodney called after Carl, "Mission accomplished, Carl. We captured the culprit."

The four of them escorted the baron back to the stable courtyard, taking care not to brush against his back. When they reached the stable, Larry met them and said, "I haven't seen Dreaddrick." He then added with a grimace, "What is that horrible smell?"

"The baron didn't have time to bathe before our meeting. Since he is a stickler for being prompt, he decided to come as he was. You know, mismatched boots, fancy black velvet with white fur trimmed pants, old dirty shirt, and barnyard perfume. His idea of regal attire," said Rodney.

Their hour deadline had come and gone. The sun was ready to peak over the horizon. The wizard was nowhere to be seen.

CHAPTER 37

"Fee fie foe fum. I smell a barnyard bum," laughed Dreaddrick looking down on the men assembled in the stable courtyard and at the baron in particular. He had suddenly appeared and was standing atop one of the huge boulders across from the stables. "Nelson, you have amused me more these past few days than anyone has in over one hundred years," stated the wizard as he continued chuckling and shaking his head from side to side.

The sun began to rise over the horizon. The men were exhausted. "Dreaddrick, we need to sit and rest for a few minutes. Shall we move into the stalls and sit on some hay bales?" asked Larry.

"Be my guest. I am in a good mood thanks to your friend," he said nodding toward their captive. "In addition, my spell book will be returned to me shortly, so I am in an extremely generous frame of mind," said the wizard as he lifted himself off the boulder and swooped ahead of them into the stable, his feet never touching the ground.

The horses had been untethered from the fence last evening and returned to their stalls, the saddles, and blankets put away. As the first stall was filled with equipment, the only other free stall was the third stall they used before. Andrew and Hans pulled several hay bales to the stall so that they could sit on something other than the hay strewn floor.

After they all made themselves as comfortable as possible, given the quarters and the circumstances, the wizard began by looking at the baron and saying, "Since you stole my spell book and claim to still have it in your possession, produce it now."

The baron, playing for time to figure a way out of this situation without having the wizard's wrath aimed directly at him, said, "You know it is in my possession. Let this stranger named Carl bring forth the spell book immediately or pay the consequences."

"Yes, we do have your spell book, Dreaddrick, but as we advised you last night, we have several conditions we wish you to meet before we hand it over," replied Carl.

"What are your requests?" asked the wizard impatiently. Clearly, Dreaddrick's good mood was slowly disappearing.

"First and foremost, Princess Charlotte must be allowed to return to her father's castle in Alauria, unharmed and without haste," said Carl.

"That wish may be granted, if you truly produce my spell book," said Dreaddrick.

"Secondly, Baron Nelson should be severely punished for kidnapping the princess," said Carl.

"That, too, I will gladly do," said Dreaddrick. "If he doesn't have the book, I look forward to taking care of the baron in several ways. My plans will be beyond his worst fears to pay him back for his treatment of me since he stole the spell book."

"But I told you! I have the book!" said the baron loudly. "Do not even entertain any punishment to me! They are the ones who deserve severe discipline imposed upon, not me!"

"Be quiet!" yelled the wizard glaring at Baron Nelson. "Let them finish with their list of requirements if they produce the book."

"Castle Grimalka is to be reverted to Gladstone Castle with all its previous refinement and beauty, such as gardens, fountains, statues, colorful pennants, and tapestries," said Larry.

"Yes, and the thick thorny vines all around the castle eliminated," added Rodney.

"The moat with electric eels and quicksand to be replaced with clear blue water filled with beautiful goldfish," said Carl.

"And many swans to swim in the moat too," said Rodney.

"Black Forest is to be replaced with the original lush green wooded lands filled with happy deer, rabbits, turtles, raccoons..." started Carl before he was interrupted by Dreaddrick who said, "Yes, yes. I know what you want. Everything back the way it was before Baron Nelson had me cast a spell over it to protect Castle Grimalka."

"Including the Near-Dead Swamp," said Carl.

"All will be granted. In fact, I will make Gladstone Castle even more glorious than it was before," said Dreaddrick.

"I too have some conditions I would like to impose without any arguments from any of you," said Dreaddrick.

"What are they?" asked Carl and Larry at the same time.

"Negotiate all you want," interrupted the baron. "I can take you to the spell book, so all this talk is for naught."

"Interesting," said Dreaddrick. "Take us to the book immediately or suffer the consequences." Dreaddrick had believed Carl when he said he had recovered the book from the baron, especially when he could describe the book in such detail, but the baron may have found where Carl secreted it and actually stolen it back. Therefore, since the wizard just wanted his precious spell book returned to him, and now, he decided to let the baron produce it and get all these negotiations over with.

"But I have a few conditions to be met," said the baron.

"Oh, all right, go ahead and tell me," sighed the wizard.

"First, I want to be wedded to Princess Charlotte before nightfall. Second, Castle Grimalka and its surroundings, the Black Forest and Near-Dead Swamp shall all remain with the enchantment you placed on them," demanded Baron Nelson.

"Most importantly, I want Carl and all his friends tortured beyond belief, and then all of them beheaded in the villagers' courtyard in a large public celebration. All of them beheaded, except Carl, of course. I haven't decided exactly how I want to finish him off yet. It will be public though, and it will be vile," the baron gloated while glaring at Carl. "We can start by placing you in the Iron Maiden with the knives protruding inside it while waiting for your public execution."

The baron then turned toward Dreaddrick putting his hands on his waist. "Then I want you to insure that I will be His Royal Highness King Nelson, ruler of all Alauria!" insisted Baron Nelson. "Above all, I desire to have you remain as my personal wizard and perform all my requests without hesitation!"

"I shall grant several of your requests, but not all," said Dreaddrick.

"You may wed your princess. I will leave the enchantments over the castle and the grounds as they are now. But you can dispose of these men as you see fit. And by marrying the princess, you will eventually become ruler of Alauria without any assistance from me," said the wizard looking with a no-nonsense glare directly at the baron's eyes.

"More importantly than any of your requests is *my* request," said Dreaddrick emphatically. "You *must* return my spell book to me, or I will do as I see fit regarding all your conditions, and you won't like my actions, dear baron,"

"Of course, Dreaddrick," agreed Baron Nelson.

CHAPTER 38

"Follow me," said the baron walking out of the stall, down the center aisle of the stable and into the morning sunlight.

He thought he knew exactly where Carl secreted the spell book. Last night he followed Carl who was walking in the direction of the hen house.

The baron led the group past the sheep corral and then the cow corral. He carefully avoided the manure pile he fell into last night. He then passed the pigpen and stopped directly in front of the hen house.

Hans and Andrew lagged far behind the others. "It'll be easy to catch up with them. Just follow the smell," said Andrew laughing. Both Hans and Andrew were almost positive that the baron could not have the spell book because Carl, Larry, and Rodney would not be so outspoken with their demands if they didn't have it themselves. Besides, the hen house was too small for such a large crowd, and they could see exactly where the baron was headed.

The hen house was a simple wooden structure with a ten-foot-high peak running from front to back. It was very large for a chicken coop and held about one hundred nesting boxes and roosts for the hens. The aisle between the boxes was not very wide and not large enough to hold even a small crowd of people. The floor was strewn with hay to collect the chicken droppings and to allow for easy clean up. Since the sun had already risen, most of the hens were already in the outside area of the coop and not sitting on their nesting boxes in the hen house.

Upon reaching the doorway to the hen house, the baron stopped and said, "The book is hidden in one of the hens' nesting boxes."

"Which one!" the wizard demanded.

"I have forgotten exactly which nest as it was dark, and I was in a hurry to hide it at the time," responded the baron.

He walked to the closest nesting spot and brushed the hen off her eggs and then tossed the nest, eggs, and all to the floor. Even though there was a thick layer of straw covering the floor, the eggs managed to break.

Dreaddrick was impatient and not about to stand here and watch the baron tear the entire chicken coop apart in search of a non-existent hidden location. "You have five minutes to find my book and bring it out here to me," roared the wizard. He turned and walked to the pigpens. Carl, Larry, and Rodney stayed outside peering through the open door knowing that the baron was on a fool's mission.

"Hey, stop!" harshly said Hans as he rushed past Carl and his friends and walked into the hen house. "You can't destroy the nesting boxes and break all the eggs!" He grabbed the baron's arm as the baron was pulling the third nest apart.

"Out of my way!" yelled the baron pushing Hans back.

Carl and Rodney rushed in and each grabbed one of the baron's arms. "Let Hans lift all the nests," demanded Larry from the doorway.

"You can stand here, calmly, in the middle of the aisle with us while Hans checks each and every nest for you," said Carl evenly to the baron.

"Or you can just get out now," added Rodney.

The baron struggled from their grasp for a few seconds and then acquiesced. "All right! But I will not budge until the book is unearthed," he replied gruffly.

Hans, accompanied by Andrew, who walked into the hen house after Rodney, both gently lifted every nest one at a time and announced after doing so that there was nothing under it. They held each nest up high enough for the baron to see it truly had nothing secreted under it. The few hens that had been in the hen house when the men arrived were very flustered and literally ran over the men's boots and out to the coop area surrounding the hen house.

Hans picked up the broken eggs and discarded nest and placed the nest back where it belonged, tossing the broken eggs into one of the egg gathering baskets hanging on a hook by the door.

"As you can plainly see, Baron, there is no book hidden in here," stated Larry as Carl and Rodney were pulling the baron out of the hen house door.

"Wait!" It must be hidden under the hay on the floor," said the baron desperately. He tried to kick at the hay on the floor with this mismatched boots while being ushered out the door.

"It is in here somewhere! I know it is! Carl was headed here last night to..." said the baron looking wide-eyed.

"Enough," declared the wizard leaning against the pigpen and watching this little farce being acted out by the baron.

"It is clear that the baron not only does not have the spell book in his possession, but he has absolutely no clue as to where it was hidden by Carl," said Larry.

CHAPTER 39

They all returned to the stables, dragging the baron reluctantly in the middle of them.

"Baron, it gives me great pleasure to finally have the opportunity to repay you for your theft of my spell book and all that you forced me to do on your behalf," the wizard said angrily while glaring at the baron.

"Now before anything further, I *want* my spell book produced and handed to me, or you *all* will be punished!" said the wizard, thoroughly out of patience.

"Will all our terms be met?" asked Larry.

"Yes. I gave my word," said the wizard.

"You were about to tell us your demands before we went on that wild goose chase with the baron," said Carl.

"Yes, what are they?" asked Rodney.

"First, I will return to my home that is far away from here and take the baron with me," began the wizard.

"But…" interrupted Carl, afraid that the baron may not be punished.

"Do not worry, Carl. You are probably afraid that I will not punish the baron. Believe me! I will make sure he is severely and thoroughly brought to task. I just want time to read through my spell book to find the harshest punishment that exists," stated Dreaddrick.

"Good," replied Carl.

"I also wish to take the fifty royal guards from Grimalka with me. They were my personal army before the baron insisted I turn them into human form and make them his royal guards."

"What type of creatures were they before you transformed them?" asked Larry.

"Since you are so curious, I shall show you," said the wizard. He then drew his wand from his pocket, raised it into the air and brought it down out in front of him, and aimed it directly at the baron. The wizard murmured several words the men could not really distinguish and that they probably never would have heard before.

A loud *zap* was heard, and the baron disappeared. In his place stood a four-foot-high ugly creature with extremely long armlike appendages that nearly reached the floor. Sharp talons were seen at the tips of these. It had a grotesque head that was wrinkled and hairless. Its eyes were jet black and shaped like two perfectly round marbles. The nose was huge in width and length and took up more than half its face area. There were no eyebrows. The mouth was cruel looking and long, extremely sharp teeth protruded out over the thin almost nonexistent lips. Its ears were very long, thinly tapered, and pointed at the top while large and rounded at the lobe area, which almost rested on its huge shoulders. Its outer covering while similar to the coloring of a sick pig it was not exactly skin-like nor was it scalelike, but something in between both. Its feet were huge and hairy. Thankfully it was clad in a beige shirtwaist type of clothing that ran from its shoulders to just above its ankles because the men could only imagine what the body of a being like this would be like. It probably had some form of tail, but the men didn't care if it did or not. They didn't want to see it.

"This is what the baron looks like in his natural form," stated the wizard. "The entire royal guard contingency is exactly the same as this creature. After he stole my spell book, he demanded that I turn him into human form and give him Gladstone Castle, or he wouldn't return my spell book. He had me enchant the Green Forest and Cypress Swamp into the Black Forest and Near-Dead Swamp to protect his castle. Nelson needed royal guards and requested I cast a spell over his fellow beings and transform them into human form too."

The wizard then looked directly at Carl and said, "I assure you that all the requests you made of me before shall be granted as I promised you immediately upon you returning my spell book."

Larry, Carl, Rodney, Hans, and Andrew were still staring in astonishment at the creature standing before them.

Carl shook his head to clear it and said to Rodney, "Please retrieve the spell book and bring it here."

Rodney immediately left the stall, walked to the first stall, and pulled the spell book from its hiding place in the bucket on the wall. Rodney picked up the blanket along with the book. He wrapped the horse blanket completely around it and walked back to the third stall.

"I didn't ask for a horse blanket. Bring me my spell book," said the wizard staring at Rodney in disbelief.

Rodney handed the horse blanket to Carl and said, "You earned the right to present the book to Dreaddrick, Carl."

Carl unwrapped the spell book and tossed the blanket aside. He looked down at the book and thought that all that had happened to them and so many other people was because of that ugly creature standing before them stealing something that didn't belong to it.

"As we have your word that all our conditions will be met, Dreaddrick, may I on behalf of everyone in this room, everyone human I should say, present you with your spell book," said Carl grandly.

"Thank you, Carl. Thank you, Lord Lawrence, Sir Rodney, Hans, and you too, Andrew," said the wizard looking at each of them in turn.

"He knows my name. He knows who we all are," said Hans in astonishment.

"Would you do us all a favor, Dreaddrick?" asked Carl.

"Another one, Carl?" asked Dreaddrick.

"Yes, and it is an important one," replied Carl. "When you perform your spells to put everything aright, would you please do so while standing in a dark room and not in daylight? You don't seem to be perfectly on the mark in sunlight," stated Carl.

"How wise of you to say so," replied the wizard with surprisingly good humor.

The men looked back and forth at each other that the wizard took what Carl said so nicely.

The wizard said with a slight chuckle, "When Nelson stole my spell book, I was on a quest for certain potions to help my eyesight. You see, after several hundred years, one's eyesight starts to fail a little. I managed to bring all the vials listed in the spell book back to my home, but not knowing the exact dosage of each, I could not mix them together. Too much or too little of the wrong potion, and I would be permanently blind. I have also lost most of my special vision so I couldn't find the spell book on my own. I have you all to thank and for which I shall forever be grateful."

The men all looked at Carl. He was correct in his assessment of Dreaddrick's vision problem.

"I will leave now and take Nelson with me. Do not fear. I shall return by midnight after mixing the potion for my eyesight and restoring same fully. If you will all meet me here then, I shall grant all your conditions. I would rather not take the chance on making any irreparable damage to any of them due to impaired vision," said the wizard with a smile.

"We agree that it would be much better if you could see clearly," said Larry, smiling back at the wizard.

"Instead of meeting at the stable, could we meet at the great dining hall instead?" asked Carl. "We want to show you something."

"Granted. Midnight at the great dining hall," said the wizard. He then raised his wand, and after a loud *schwum* was heard, both he and the ugly creature, formerly Baron Nelson, disappeared from sight.

CHAPTER 40

The men immediately walked through the tunnel and to the kitchens.

"Where have you all been?" asked Frederick frantically.

"Why are you so upset?" asked Larry.

"So many things have happened. It is unbelievable. First, the royal guards in the cellars all transformed into some ugly creatures, completely indescribable hideous things. Then within minutes, they all just disappeared from the cellars altogether, every single one of them. It was as if they never existed," said Frederick with a worried look on his face.

"That's right, my friend. They never did exist," said Carl calmly.

"We have to disappear now too," said Rodney. They had a lot to attend to right now.

"You have absolutely nothing to worry about, Frederick. The creatures will never return to the castle again," advised Larry.

"In either their human or creature form," added Paul.

"Will you and all the villagers join us in the great dining hall at midnight?" asked Carl.

"We will explain everything to everybody then," said Larry.

"I will spread the word immediately. Do you wish to have dinner served there at midnight? We have the entire wedding celebration dinner already prepared, and it would be a shame to waste it," said Frederick.

"That would be perfect," said Rodney.

"Thank you, Frederick," said Larry over his shoulder as the men were leaving the kitchens.

Carl told Hans to find the princess's lady-in-waiting and have her await the princess in her bedchambers with a nice hot bath and fresh clothing.

Andrew was sent to the great dining hall to try to repair his uncle's masonry work so no one would trip and fall over the pile of blocks left in the center of the room. Rodney volunteered to help Andrew and also bring some of the villagers with him to help.

Carl looked all around the courtyard and didn't see Jake. He didn't really think Jake would be in the courtyard with a real princess staying in his home, but he thought he'd look anyway. So Carl and Larry climbed the stairs to Lily's home. Paul was standing sentry duty outside with Billy happily sitting at his feet, playing with his marbles.

When Carl and Larry entered the doors, Carl saw the princess sitting on a bench with a smile on her face, listening to Jake babble on about something, very excitedly. Lily was clearing the table of breakfast dishes.

"Hello, all," said Carl.

"Good morning," said Larry.

Jake ran to Carl and hugged him around the waist and said with great enthusiasm, "The princess and I are talking about games to play. She is really very special."

"Jake hasn't stopped talking since you left last night. I don't think the princess had a wink of sleep," said Lily gently nodding her head side to side.

"We have good news and would like to share some of it with you all now," said Larry.

"Jake, ask Sir Paul to come inside and have him bring Billy with him," said Carl.

Larry said he would stand watch for a while although it probably was not necessary now. Therefore, after Paul and Billy came inside, Larry went outside and left the door open so he could hear what Carl imparted to them.

Carl decided not to tell them all the details but just the important parts. The rest they would learn when they were all assembled at the midnight feast.

Billy, Jake, Lily, and the princess were seated at the table. Paul and Carl sat on the straw mattresses and faced them.

"The baron has permanently left Castle Grimalka and will never return," announced Carl.

The princess immediately smiled with the largest smile Carl had ever seen. She was absolutely delighted. Lily and Jake both laughed and were clearly very happy too. Billy said, "Does that mean I don't have to make any more pennants or have to get dressed up for a party?"

"Yes, Billy," answered Carl with a grin.

"Princess Charlotte, your lady-in-waiting is in your bedchambers preparing a fresh bath for you to relax in. After that, you are instructed to take a real long nap and wake up refreshed for a midnight feast. Everyone in the village will be at the feast. We have a special guest coming, and it will be marvelous," said Carl.

The princess did not mind having someone give her orders when they were exactly what she wanted to do anyway.

"A long leisurely bath and a full nap sound heavenly right now, especially when topped off with a midnight feast," said the princess with a glow on her face.

Larry and Paul escorted the princess to her bedchamber after she thanked Lily, Jake, and Billy for entertaining her so graciously. She also told them that she wanted the three of them to be seated at her table with her at the feast tonight. Everyone was elated.

Carl stayed behind to talk to Lily and the boys.

"I can't thank you enough for all you have done for me and especially for the princess," said Carl to Lily.

"And also you, Jake, and you too, Billy, have been wonderful. I am proud of you both," said Carl, ruffling Billy's bright red hair and patting Jake on the back.

"Billy, I am sorry, but you *must* attend the feast tonight. Do as the princess is doing and take a nap later this afternoon so you can stay awake for the festivities," said Carl.

"I want to go tonight, Will," said Jake excitedly. "Will we really be seated with the princess at the main table?"

"Yes, you will, Jake. And, my name is really Carl, not Will," he said.

"Really?" asked Jake.

"Yes, I am afraid so," apologized Carl.

"You will understand everything tonight," Carl said. "In the meantime, I am exhausted and must take a nap myself."

"You can lay right down there on Jake's mat, Carl. But first, I will prepare a small breakfast for you. Then you take as long a nap as you like," said Lily.

"That sounds wonderful," said Carl gratefully.

CHAPTER 41

Around nine o'clock, Carl awoke feeling refreshed and very happy. He had dreamed of the beautiful Princess Charlotte and replayed her sweet kiss on his cheek over and over again. It was the best dream he had in a long time.

Lily was sitting on one of the benches close to the candlelight mending a pair of boy's pants. Both Jake and Billy were sleeping soundly on Billy's mat.

Carl arose from the straw mat and whispered to Lily that he had to take leave now but that he was looking forward to seeing her and the boys at the midnight feast in the great dining hall. Lily nodded in response and returned to her darning.

Carl immediately went to the great dining hall to see how the repair work on the stone floor was coming along. Andrew and the villagers had managed to replace the now broken gray background stones with new white stones.

He spotted Larry and Paul sleeping on benches.

"Don't wake them, Carl," said Andrew. "They worked very hard all afternoon. Hans and the villagers went to the old quarry and brought back white stone to replace the old gray stone in the floor emblem. Larry stayed here to help me work on the stone floor while we filled Paul in on what happened with the baron and the wizard. Then they joined Hans and the villagers to work at the quarry and bring the last load of white stone back here. It is backbreaking work."

"Where is Hans now?" asked Carl.

"He and several villagers are at the quarry loading up red stones. Larry thought that since we were rebuilding the floor, we could surprise the princess tonight with a red rose instead of a black rose in the emblem," said Andrew.

"Will you be able to complete the work before the midnight feast?" asked Carl.

"We will be cutting it close, but when Hans returns, Larry asked me to wake them up to help finish the floor," replied Andrew.

"Excellent!" exclaimed Carl.

"Where is the quarry?" asked Carl.

"The quarry is behind the castle vegetable gardens. It is quite far off, and it took five villagers as well as Larry, Paul, and Hans to load up and pull the wagons through the tunnel and around the court-yards. Luckily, my Uncle Douglas had trained two villagers how to cut the stone before he retired," said Andrew.

"Apparently you were an excellent apprentice of your uncle's," observed Carl seeing the perfect finishing work Andrew was applying to the stone he was laying in the floor.

"Thank you," beamed Andrew in reply.

"I see that I may leave now since this project is in good hands," said Carl as he walked toward the door.

Carl was anxious to see how the princess was feeling. She has gone through more than any princess should ever see in many life-times. It was a relief to see Rodney rather than the royal guards stand-ing sentry duty in the hallway outside the princess's bedchambers.

Upon seeing Carl walking toward him, Rodney said, "Princess Charlotte's lady-in-waiting just entered her chambers carrying a fresh gown for this evening's festivities."

Laughter could be heard through the closed door. It was music to Carl's ears.

"Hans has arranged for a bath and fresh clothing to be brought for all of us to the room across the hall," said Rodney, smiling. "Go in and prepare yourself for tonight. You can relieve me when you are finished."

When Carl opened the door, he saw two villagers laying cloth-ing across the four-poster bed. As soon as one of the villagers saw Carl, he smiled broadly and motioned for Carl to sit down on the settee by the roaring fire ablaze in the huge fireplace. As one villager started to remove Carl's boots, the other villager left the room for hot water. Within minutes, two villagers brought steaming hot water in large buckets and poured same into the vast wooden tub that had been placed in the center of the room. They assisted Carl out of his dirty clothing and into the tub. The hot water felt so relaxing to Carl, especially after they poured some special soothing oils in the tub.

When the water cooled, two villagers helped Carl from the tub as the third wrapped him in a luxurious oversized towel. They proceeded to dress him in a white silk shirt and a teal blue linen suit trimmed with white ermine fur. Boots that were shined to reflect the smallest fraction of light were placed upon his feet. Carl not only looked like but felt like a king in this well-tailored finery.

The villagers emptied the tub by ladling the water out of it and into the many empty buckets piled by the door. They then wiped the inside of the tub dry. As Carl was leaving the room, he could see another suit was being laid out on the bed and another pair of boots was being shined to a high gloss.

"I feel absolutely wonderful," said Carl to Rodney. "I will relieve you of your post, Rodney. It is your turn to be treated like a king. You deserve it."

While standing outside the princess's door, Carl felt even better hearing the laughter and happy voices coming through the door from inside the room.

When Rodney emerged later, he looked splendid in a forest green suit, also trimmed with white ermine fur. Carl asked Rodney to go to the great dining hall and see if Larry or Paul were ready to be refreshed and dressed for the night's festivities.

Within minutes, Larry and Paul both appeared before Carl. "Andrew is putting the finishing touches on the red rose and should be completed in a few minutes. Then he, Hans, and the hardworking villagers will all bathe and dress," advised Larry.

"Everything will be ready before the stroke of midnight," said Paul proudly.

Later, both Larry and Paul emerged from the bedroom looking as regal as Carl and Rodney. Larry was clad in maroon velvet with gold braid trim. Paul wore a deep purple linen suit trimmed with gray fur. The four complimented each other quite heartedly and smiled broadly.

At ten minutes to midnight, Carl knocked gently on the princess's door. A handmaiden opened the door. They could see Princess Charlotte seated on the settee by a roaring fire burning in the fireplace while her lady-in-waiting was putting the finishing touches on the princess's hair.

Princess Charlotte arose as she saw the men waiting in the hall outside her door. She was a beautiful vision in the deep blue sea gown that matched the color of her exquisite eyes. This was the dress she wore when Carl first saw her. Her long golden curls were brushed to a glorious shine that had light bouncing off in the reflected firelight. She wore the biggest, warmest smile he had ever seen.

She walked to the door and all four men immediately gave her a deep bow and said at the same time, "Your Royal Highness."

Both Larry and Carl offered the princess their arms, and she placed her right hand on Carl's left arm and her left hand on Larry's right arm. Paul and Rodney proudly walked behind them. The four men escorted the beautiful princess to the great dining hall with regal smiles on their faces and looking as if they were going to attend a formal royal ball.

CHAPTER 42

The great hall was filled with every villager, man, woman, and child as well as the minor royalty that had been guests of Baron Nelson. It was a rainbow of color in the room. No one wore black, dark brown, or dark gray. Everyone was gaily dressed. The word had been passed around that this was to be a happy celebration, and if anyone showed up in dark depressing colors, they would be turned away and not allowed to join in on the festivities.

Extra tables and benches had been brought in to accommodate such a huge crowd of people. The villagers worked hard on the preparations for the special gala, and they were proud of their efforts.

Four men managed to find some old musical instruments and were trying to play them. The music wasn't very polished, but their attempts were good enough to make everyone enjoy it.

Upon seeing the princess and her escorts, the crowd moved aside to allow them to gain access to the main table. Each person they passed gave a curtsy or bow to the princess and a broad smile to the men.

Just before the stroke of midnight, everyone was seated at the tables and talking animatedly, wondering what this celebration was all about and where was the baron. At midnight, the two huge doors at the entrance to the great dining hall were pushed open, and a hush fell over the previously noisy room. The music stopped. No one said a word. Carl looked up and saw a large silver serpent with the body like a huge lizard flying through the doors. It had bat-like wings growing from its back that were slowly raising and lowering as it came to rest on two lizard-type legs landing directly above the rose emblem. It possessed a scaly body with a row of dorsal spines running from its head down its long, long, tail. Two large round black eyes shone brightly on its face. Sharp sharklike teeth could be seen in its partially opened mouth. Sitting astride the dragon's back was the wizard, Dreaddrick, dressed in royal purple robes and hat both with silver insignias embroidered all over them.

He dismounted with a little difficulty as his robes kept getting caught on the dragon's spines, but he finally was able to put both feet on the stone floor without further mishap. The wizard then strode to the main table and looked from Paul to Larry to Princess Charlotte to Carl and finally to Rodney seated wide-eyed and with their mouths slightly open. In fact, every other person in the room had the same expressions on their faces. They had always heard tales of dragons, but no one had actually seen one until now.

"I am glad to see everyone assembled here," said Dreaddrick as he turned and looked throughout the great dining hall. He appeared to have looked each and every person, adult and child, in the eye as he glanced throughout the room.

"I have a lot of explaining to do but will only give you the highlights right now. Lord Lawrence, Sir Rodney, Sir Paul, and especially Carl will fill you in on the details as they see fit," began Dreaddrick addressing everyone.

"Of the utmost importance is to notify you that Baron Nelson has left Castle Grimalka, never to return again," began the wizard. He could see that that announcement brought a sigh of relief to all present, villagers and royal guests alike. They looked around at each other with relieved smiles on their faces.

"Major changes will be made to the castle that you will notice when you leave the great dining hall," he said with a smile. "These changes are occurring as we speak."

The guests started to murmur among themselves.

"If you have any questions, please speak with those men I mentioned before. I am tired and hungry and wish to join in on the festivities as soon as Hans and Andrew take Dudley to the stables and feed him," said the wizard looking Hans in the eye. "He is a gentle creature, I assure you, Hans, if you do not pull too hard on his leash," cautioned Dreaddrick while handing the end of a long, long rope to him.

Hans and Andrew both looked absolutely terrified. They were told to take a *dragon* to their stables!

"Hurry, lads," said the wizard.

Hans looked down at the end of the rope in his hands and looked up at Carl who was sitting at the table, smiling. He knew that the wizard would not lie to them and that Dudley was probably as gentle as a lamb...as long as he was treated delicately.

"It's okay, boys," said Carl to Hans and Andrew to reassure them.

"What does he eat?" Andrew asked Dreaddrick.

"Anything, as long as it is either still moving or freshly killed," replied the wizard. "Take Dudley through the courtyards and tunnel to the stables and see that he is fed. Then return and join us," said Dreaddrick.

Hans picked up the end of the rope and started to walk away from Dreaddrick.

"Wait! I should tell you one other thing. Don't feed him any very, very hot peppers."

"What happens if he eats hot peppers?" inquired Hans.

"Dudley loves them, so he gulps them down rapidly. Eating food too fast gives him the hiccups. When he hiccups he can't control his breath, so with each hiccup, he shoots out fire," explained Dreaddrick.

Hans and Andrew looked at each other with worried looks but started to walk to the other side of the great dining hall.

"Oh, and make sure the special fireproof rope is tied tightly so that Dudley doesn't wander off," added the wizard as Hans and Andrew were slowly leading the dragon out of the great dining hall, terror clearly written on both their faces. Hans and Andrew were looking at each other with *why me?* looks.

"Hurry back here, boys, to join in on the feast," said Larry just before the large wooden doors closed behind them.

CHAPTER 43

"Frederick, please start serving the feast if you don't mind," said Larry.

"Immediately," was Frederick's response.

People started talking among themselves in awe of both the dragon and wizard. They were elated that Baron Nelson would not return. The bright colors allowed in the castle also made them happy inside. Soon the noise level was as loud as before Dreaddrick and Dudley entered the hall.

The diners at the head table moved around in their chairs to make room for Dreaddrick to sit next to Rodney. Jake sat on one side of the princess while Larry sat on the other side of her. Lily was seated alongside of Paul, and Carl was between Paul and Larry. Billy was seated on Rodney's left. The lesser royals who were guests of the baron rounded out the revelers at the main table. There were two empty chairs, one for Hans and one for Andrew at the main table. The villagers filled the rest of the great dining hall to its full capacity.

Frederick's staff brought great amounts of broiled venison, roast pig, stewed fowl, and beef cooked in various ways with lots of special sauces and gravies. Mounds of potatoes, spinach, green beans, carrots, squash, broccoli, and other assorted vegetables were served on highly piled platters. The aroma of fresh baked bread and rolls filled the room. Fresh fruit was the second to last items to be brought out and served to them.

Goblets were filled with mead and wine. The waiters made sure that everyone's goblet was instantly refilled as they were drained by the revelers.

As Frederick and the staff were wheeling in the dessert wagons, he excitedly announced that physical changes were made to the castle from when he started serving the meats until they were bringing in the final course. He very excitedly said, "The castle looks like it did before the baron changed it all when it was Gladstone Castle, only better!"

"Wait until you finish the final course and sample many of Frederick's wonderful desserts before leaving," called out Larry as some of the villagers were eager to see what Frederick was raving about. Quite a few had already stood and started to walk away from the tables before Larry spoke. They returned to their seats, and they happily partook of the delicious delights that were being served. There were many types of cakes with all sorts of fancy toppings that they had never seen before. Each pastry looked more delicious than the one next to it.

When it seemed that most of the diners were finished, Carl stood and said, "We have a few things to relate, and then you may all be free to return to your homes."

A hush fell over the room, and all eyes turned to Carl.

"First and foremost, we would like to thank Frederick and his staff for this fantastic feast," proclaimed Carl, holding his arm out toward the beaming chef. Frederick and his staff were praised by everyone at once.

When the accolades ceased, Carl continued, "Have you noticed that there is no longer a black rose set in a gray square in the center of the emblem in the stone floor? Thanks to Andrew it has been replaced with a red rose on a white background, as have all the pennants and banners throughout Castle Gladstone." Carl looked over toward the princess who was leaning forward to look over the table at the emblem in the floor.

"I'm delighted!" exclaimed the princess with a smile in Carl's direction.

"Under the old gray square with the black rose is where Baron Nelson secreted your spell book," Rodney relayed to the wizard sitting next to him.

"Due to my failing eyesight, I could not see through the stonework," said Dreaddrick with a sigh. "How did you find it?"

"Andrew related the old stories he heard from his Uncle Douglas who had laid the original floor at the baron's instructions," said Rodney.

"And the baron dug it up and then had Douglas relay the stonework. There was no reason for it to be dug up and a new emblem put down unless the baron had hidden something he wanted to conceal under the stone floor. He wanted it secreted someplace that he could keep a constant eye on," added Larry.

"Carl is the one who figured it all out," said Paul proudly.

CHAPTER 44

Hans and Andrew were both excited beyond belief when they returned to the great dining hall.

"It's fantastic!" said Hans out of breath.

"Everyone, come and see!" said Andrew, also out of breath. Both men had run the entire way from the stables through the tunnel, cutting through the kitchens to the courtyard and into the hall. They were so excited that they managed to run the entire distance in less than five minutes.

Larry and the princess were the first to follow Hans while Rodney, Paul, and Carl followed Andrew. They pushed through the crowd of villagers smiling and saying, "Follow us," as they passed them.

Every lantern in the courtyards was lit. The old lanterns were replaced with beautiful ornate black wrought iron lanterns. The old wooden homes and stairs were gone, and in their place stood stone houses and stone steps. All the doors were wide open and roaring fires in fireplaces were glimpsed through the doors. But the biggest change in front of them was the main courtyard itself.

Instead of hard packed dirt, the courtyard was now comprised of stonework in pretty patterns. A large flowing fountain adorned the center of the courtyard surrounded by assorted flowers of every type and color. There were round stone tables with curved stone benches scattered throughout the open area. Flowers hung in baskets from the balconies. Topiaries in the shapes of forest animals such as rabbits and deer were next to every staircase. Each topiary was surrounded with an array of flowers in a different color scheme from the other topiaries. Even by candlelight the courtyard was magical.

The drawbridge courtyard was no longer drab and empty. All the large boulders had disappeared. The drawbridge gates had been made of dark, thick wood but now shone brightly with golden gates in intricate designs.

Even the smaller kitchen courtyard by the tunnel had been magically transformed to a beautiful area. Again, ornate black wrought iron lanterns were hanging on the walls. Inlaid stonework covered the entire courtyard. Baskets overflowing with colorful flowers were scattered throughout.

The villagers were awestruck and happier than they ever were.

Larry climbed the nearest set of stairs and looked down at the contented villagers. He announced, "In addition to the baron leaving, the royal guards have gone, also never to return. We need good men who wish to be trained in swordsmanship and horsemanship to become Castle Gladstone's royal guard. If any of you so desire, please let Sir Rodney here know." Rodney had followed Larry up the stairs, and Larry now put his arm across Rodney's back. "Sir Rodney will live in Castle Gladstone as your commander of the royal guards."

Cheers rang out among the villagers. Some men started to approach the staircase to volunteer before Larry could get down the stairs to the courtyard.

Dreaddrick had already climbed another set of stairs, and it was his turn to address the crowd. "In the daylight, you shall see that there are no longer any thick black thorny vines encompassing the castle."

More cheers and happy calls were heard.

"And," he continued, "the Black Forest has been changed back to the lush green friendly woods filled with happy animals and brightly colored flowers. The Near-Dead Swamp is now the Cedar Swamp and flowing with pristine clear blue water."

The villagers were completely elated.

Carl climbed the stairs and stood next to Dreaddrick and said he had one more announcement for everyone. "Lord Lawrence, Princess Charlotte, Sir Paul, Sir Rodney, and I will be leaving for Alauria and King Stephen's castle tomorrow morning. But…"

Before he could finish, the crowd was saying, "No!"

"Please don't leave!"

"You have made our lives so much better!"

"We need you all here!"

Carl had to wave both his hands up high to stop the uproar of the villagers at his announcement. When the commotion finally died down, he continued, "As you have already been advised, Sir Rodney will return here very shortly as your new royal guard commander. He has to return to Alauria to bring his wife and children to Gladstone Castle. In addition, Lord Lawrence and Princess Audrey will come here to live right after their wedding."

At that announcement, the crowd started cheering again.

CHAPTER 45

They all escorted the princess back to her bedchambers. Rodney and Paul remained as sentries at her door. None of them thought that any guard was needed, but old habits are hard to break. The rest of them returned to the stables along with Dreaddrick. They needed a full night's sleep for tomorrow's journey.

It took them quite a while to get from the princess's bedchambers to the stables as they were stopped every few feet to be personally thanked by the villagers. Some had already returned to their new stone homes where the old wooden ones were and came out to tell them how happy their families were, especially with real fireplaces and actual beds instead of open firepits and straw mattresses on the floor.

Dudley was tethered to the stable fence and was sound asleep, snoring loudly, by the time they arrived. Larry, Carl, Dreaddrick, Hans, and Andrew all instantly fell fast asleep, and none of them awoke until well after the sun rose.

In the morning Carl and Larry, being the last ones to awaken, were told by Hans to climb the boulder and look at Cedar Swamp which they happily did. It was beautiful! The sun shone through the cedar trees and reflected light of silver and gold on the water. Happy animals were seen playing in the wooded area. A turtle was sunning itself on a rock. Flowers showed off their beautiful colors on both the water and on the land. Large white water lilies on bright green leaves were scattered on the surface of the clear blue water. Birds were flying around and tweeting cheerfully. It was hard to believe that only yesterday it was Near-Dead Swamp.

When they climbed down off the boulder, Hans told them that breakfast was ready. Frederick had prepared and sent them food from the kitchens. After finishing off a delicious repast of bacon, eggs, freshly baked bread, and a variety of fruit, the men began to pack up their tools and weapons to make ready for their journey home.

Dreaddrick offered Dudley to Larry so that they could quickly fly home and would not have to spend many days on horseback, but they all refused his gracious offer. Not one of them wanted to ride on a dragon's back for one minute much less one whole day. Declining, they thanked Dreaddrick and began to saddle some horses.

"Since you do not wish to take advantage of Dudley to return you to Alauria, I have left some other means of travel for you at the drawbridge courtyard," said Dreaddrick.

They thanked him for everything he had done for the princess, them, and the villagers. But before they left, they extracted a promise from Dreaddrick that he would be the official wizard of Alauria and advise them and aid them as needed.

"I will continue to live in my home far over the mountains, but you only have to call out my name, and I shall return to assist you in any way I can. I will always be grateful to each of you for returning my spell book to me," said Dreaddrick with gratitude in his voice.

Carl and Larry said their goodbyes to Hans and Andrew and promised them they would return to Gladstone Castle shortly.

After collecting Princess Charlotte, Rodney, and Paul, they decided to return to the kitchens to say goodbye to Frederick and his cooks.

Carl then ran up to see Lily, Jake, and Billy. When Lily opened the door, Carl could see the change in their quarters. It was larger than the old house. There were three beds where the straw mats had lain. Colorful curtains adorned a huge window that overlooked the transformed courtyard below. The firepit in the middle of the room was gone, and a large stone fireplace was on the far wall, with a warming fire lit inside. Where the firepit had been situated a large thick oval rug with pretty designs lay in its place. Over the fireplace were several hooks. One was holding a large cast iron kettle that was filled with a bubbling stew. The aroma was wonderful.

Lily, Jake, and Billy all thanked Carl for making everyone's lives so much better. The villagers were finally happy again.

Jake and Billy were sorry to see Carl leave, but he promised he would return to Gladstone Castle very soon. The boys insisted on accompanying Carl and the others to the drawbridge gate and say goodbye to Larry, Paul, and the princess too.

CHAPTER 46

They all met in the courtyard by the new flowing fountain. The courtyard was filled with lots of happy villagers waving goodbye to them.

Before they left, Carl said he had one more thing to do. He quickly strode through the kitchens and the tunnel to the stables. He arrived just as Dreaddrick was climbing onto Dudley's back.

"Wait!" called out Carl. "I have a very special favor to ask of you, Dreaddrick. This is extremely important."

Dreaddrick dismounted Dudley and walked over to Carl. "What is so important?" he asked.

When Carl told him, Dreaddrick nodded his head rapidly in an affirmative manner. He followed Carl back through the tunnel and the kitchen to the inner courtyard. They stopped at the fountain and stood in front of Jake and Billy.

"Here is Billy," said Carl. Billy was sitting on the bench nearest the fountain.

Dreaddrick extracted his wand from his pocket, held it in Billy's direction, and said a few words that no one could understand.

"Billy, come over here," demanded the wizard.

"I can't walk, sir," was Billy's reply.

"I said, 'come over here,' Billy," stated the wizard even louder.

Jake stood up and looked Dreaddrick in his eyes. He summoned all the courage he could and said, "My brother is crippled, and he can't walk."

"I am not talking to you. I am talking to Billy," said Dreaddrick glaring back at Jake.

Jake took a big gulp and figured he better help Billy do as the wizard requested. He put his arm around Billy so he could stand up and the wizard could see that Billy couldn't walk. Jake dropped his arm off his brother and looked at the wizard as if to say, *"I told you he couldn't walk."*

"Come here, Billy," said the wizard ignoring Jake's glare.

As Billy stood facing the wizard, he moved his right foot forward a few inches. He looked down in amazement at his feet and then proceeded to move his left foot forward. That one, too, inched forward at his will. A slow smile started on Billy's face as he looked up toward Dreaddrick, and then he walked a few more steps and started to cry.

"I can walk," said Billy softly in disbelief as tears began to flow down his cheek.

"I can walk! I can walk!" Billy said boldly. He then yelled as loudly as he could. *"I can walk!"*

Billy walked as quickly as his newly found movable legs could take him and rushed to Dreaddrick's side. He threw his arms around the wizard and gave him a huge hug while tears ran down his face.

Jake happily ran for his mother and brought her to the courtyard. She started crying as loudly as Billy.

The villagers crowded around the wizard, Billy, Jake, and Lily, many with tears of joy running off their cheeks.

Carl thanked Dreaddrick and said they now must leave.

Upon rounding the corner to the drawbridge courtyard, the princess stopped and caught her breath. An elegant carriage stood directly in front of the new golden gates. It had four large wheels. A team of six white horses each with a large red plume on its head were harnessed to the front of the carriage. It was elaborately decorated and gilded in gold. There was room for storing their packs in a small covered area behind the interior seating area. The seating inside the carriage consisted of one double seat facing forward and one double seat facing backward. The seats were covered with thick soft black leather. Two fur-lined white blankets were placed on the seats. Red velvet drapery was rolled up above the windows on the interior to be let down to keep out weather, sun, or simply for privacy. Dreaddrick had left them with an extremely nice going away present.

Rodney and Paul immediately climbed up onto the front of the carriage and grabbed the reins while Larry and Carl stowed the packs in the boot. Larry then rushed to the princess to assist her into climbing inside the carriage. By the time all five of them were ensconced in the carriage and ready to leave, Jake, Billy, and Lily had rounded the corner from the inner courtyard. The three of them stood and waved as the carriage rolled across the drawbridge and toward the lush Green Forest where the Black Forest once stood. They looked down at the moat while on the drawbridge and saw large goldfish swimming in the clear blue water. Swans were gracefully gliding across the moat.

The carriage stopped on the other side of the drawbridge so that they could take a look at Gladstone Castle and the new white pennants with one red rose on each. It was a wondrous sight.

CHAPTER 47

The journey back was a good one. The gilded carriage was extremely comfortable as well as beautiful. As they rode through the countryside, they were greeted by farmers and villagers with happy waves.

The best part of the entire journey home was when they were riding through the old Black Forest. Where it previously had been completely black and depressing, it was now green, lush, and beautiful. They saw something none of them had ever seen before: a unicorn. It was a magical sight. The unicorn was white with a large pointed spiraling white horn in the middle of its forehead. It was drinking from the clear blue brook in the middle of the forest. The unicorn looked up and directly at them as they rode past. Carl was positive the unicorn was smiling.

They were relieved to be free and extremely happy that Baron Nelson would never return. They were happier still that Gladstone Castle had been reverted to its former glory; in fact, much better than it ever was.

*****

King Stephen was elated when they arrived at his castle. As soon as the golden carriage pulled through the new Green Forest, the king's royal guards who were posted outside the old Black Forest had swiftly ridden ahead to let everyone prepare for their arrival at Alauria.

Lord Lawrence was anxious to see Princess Audrey. Sir Rodney wanted to prepare his family for their moving to Gladstone Castle and him becoming commander of the royal guards there. Sir Paul was happy to return to his royal guard unit in Alauria.

King Stephen promoted Sir Paul to commander of Alauria's royal guards as Sir Rodney was leaving them for Gladstone Castle.

Carl had missed Tommy and all his woodland friends and told King Stephen that he had to go home immediately. King Stephen let him leave on the promise that he would return for Princess Audrey and Lord Lawrence's nuptials. Carl was glad to agree as he not only desired to attend the wedding he also wanted an excuse to see Princess Charlotte again.

When the drawbridge was lowered to let Carl go home, he was amazed to see that the twenty-foot-high hedge between Alauria and his woods was gone. King Stephen had taken it down so that Carl would be able to come and go between the castle and his home.

The birds were flying overhead and tweeting happy sounds. All the animals were pleased to see him, especially Tommy, his cat. Tommy rushed up to Carl, gave a loud "meow," and brushed completely around Carl's legs. Carl leaned over and picked him up. Tommy had a good time with Sally and Arnold Chipmunk and their family. Mrs. Chipmunk was a good mother and kept them all safe and happy. But Carl still missed every one very much. He even missed Sammy the Skunk.

*****

Several days after returning home, Sir Paul knocked on Carl's door. He was dressed in his royal guard military uniform of royal blue with white trim and was wearing his white belt around his waist with a sheathed sword. He wore a royal blue hat festooned with a large white feather.

"Why are you dressed so formally, Sir Paul?" asked Carl with a smile on his face. He was glad to see Paul.

"I am here on royal duty," replied Sir Paul. "King Stephen requests your presence at the marriage of Lord Lawrence and Princess Audrey tomorrow afternoon."

"I will gladly attend the wedding," replied Carl. He was looking forward to seeing Lord Lawrence and Princess Audrey wedded, but more importantly, he wished to see Princess Charlotte one more time.

Hearing a commotion outside his door, Carl opened it wide. Standing in the clearing was Tommy with all his forest animal friends clustered behind him.

Carl said to Sir Paul, "I promised everyone that I would tell them about my adventure tomorrow morning. But when they saw you in your royal guard uniform, they wanted to know what was happening and could not wait until tomorrow."

The animals all moved closer to Carl's opened door with hopeful looks on their faces.

"Do you have time to join us? They would like to hear all about you too," said Carl beckoning Sir Paul to come outside with him.

"I would be delighted," replied Sir Paul.

Both Carl and Sir Paul sat down on some large logs that Carl had not yet cut up for firewood. Tommy jumped onto Carl's lap and settled down comfortably. The forest animals arranged themselves in a semicircle in front of the men. They were very curious about the man in his splendid uniform, so Carl started by introducing Sir Paul.

"This gentleman seated next to me in his regal military uniform is Sir Paul, commander of King Stephen's royal guard in Alauria. He accompanied me on my adventure," began Carl.

He then introduced Sir Paul to Sammy Skunk, Jill and Bill Deer and their son Ricky, Chester the Elderly Turtle, Raymond Raccoon, Betsy Badger, Peter Porcupine, Mrs. Chipmunk and her children, Sally and Arnold. The animals were very impressed that a real knight was here talking to them.

A few minutes after the introductions were completed, several other of their animal friends joined them, as well as at least twenty of their feathered friends. Carl promised to introduce the late stragglers after they finished their tale.

Carl told them all about the beautiful Princess Charlotte with sparkling eyes the color of the deep blue sea, long golden curls, and the biggest, warmest smile he had ever seen. The forest animals "ooohhhed" and "aaahhhed" over his descriptions of the beautiful princess. He then told them that she had been abducted by an evil baron.

Neither Carl nor Sir Paul wanted to upset these sweet animal friends, so they only spoke about the lush Green Forest, Cedar Swamp, and Gladstone Castle in their current beauty. They did not mention the Black Forest, the Near-Dead Swamp, nor did they describe the evil baron or the royal guard creatures and their dastardly deeds.

"We rode on a beautiful white silver-winged horse," said Carl. "We flew high up in the sky just like the cardinals and blue jays do here in the forest."

"We saw a magical unicorn in the lush Green Forest," added Sir Paul. "He really had a single large horn in the center of his forehead."

In the middle of their tales, Tommy jumped off Carl's lap and onto Sir Paul's lap. Carl was impressed that Tommy considered Sir Paul a good friend.

Carl went on to mention Hans, the stable master, and Andrew, the stone mason, as well as Frederick, the great chef. He described where they worked in great detail telling them about the kitchens, stables, hen house, sheep pens, pigsty, cattle corals, and huge vegetable gardens.

Sir Paul told them about Lily and her two sons, Jake and Billy. He said, "They play marbles and hoops, tag, and other games just like you do with your friends. Some day we will bring them here to play with you."

Sir Paul said, "Carl was the bravest man I know. He convinced a powerful wizard to help rescue the beautiful princess. And he had the wizard restore Billy's legs so that Billy is no longer a cripple but now can run and play."

Tommy jumped off Sir Paul's lap and curled up on the ground between both men while listening to the rest of the story. Tommy was very contented to have two human friends close to him.

Carl ended the tale with a description of the six beautiful white horses and the golden carriage that they rode in back to Alauria.

The animals were very impressed that King Stephen sent Carl to accompany royalty like Lord Lawrence and two of the king's knights, Sir Paul and Sir Rodney, on the quest to save the beautiful princess. They were a rapt audience for everything Carl and Sir Paul related to them.

When it turned dark, the animals returned to their homes and Carl, Sir Paul, and Tommy went back into Carl's cottage. Carl asked Sir Paul to stay overnight in his humble abode as he had preparations to attend to before leaving his home again. Sir Paul agreed, and they made plans to leave right after breakfast the following morning.

CHAPTER 48

Carl was dressed in his woodland clothing when they left his cottage. Sir Paul advised that King Stephen wanted to treat Carl to a royal pampering to thank him for all he had done to rescue Princess Charlotte.

They were greeted by King Stephen, personally, when they crossed the wooden drawbridge over the lake. The white and black swans were gliding gracefully on the lake, and it reminded Carl of the first time he crossed the drawbridge and saw the beautiful princess, the girl of his visions.

Douglas was sent for by King Stephen so that Carl could talk to him about the splendid stonework he did in Gladstone Castle. Carl also wanted to give him the good news that his nephew Andrew was to be the royal stone mason for all of Alauria. As soon as Andrew finished working on some special request stonework at Gladstone Castle, he was to be granted leave to come to King Stephen's castle and visit with Douglas. Andrew's uncle was elated and proudly told Carl that Andrew had been an excellent student and learned everything quickly and well that Douglas had taught him.

Carl was immediately ushered up the stairs to one of the guest bedchambers where four man servants were awaiting his presence. Hot water was being poured into the large tub in the middle of the room. Oils were poured into the water, and the bath was very inviting. Carl almost didn't want to get out of it. When he finished washing, he was brought a huge towel to dry himself. Clean clothing had already been laid out on a large settee for him. The shirt was pure white silk, and the jacket and pants were deep blue linen, trimmed with silver braid and were finely tailored. Again, the boots they fitted on him shone like glass. King Stephen had ordered clothing for Carl that was fit for royalty.

Sir Paul personally fetched Carl for the wedding. As they strode through the castle, there were decorations everywhere he could see. This was a very happy occasion, and the castle was never so glorious.

The pennants were attached to silver streamers that glistened in the lantern light. The royal wedding was to take place in the great hall while the festivities were to be conducted immediately after in the dining hall. Both rooms had strings of red roses hung by silver cords, and the tables were adorned with many silver vases filled with red roses.

Within minutes, people started pouring into the great hall. Carl estimated he saw over two hundred fifty guests. Everyone was decked out in gaily colored clothing. They were wearing some of the finest outfits he had seen. There was not one unsmiling face in the crowd.

King Stephen stood on the emblem in the center of the great hall. Lord Larry stood on his left side awaiting the wedding procession. The royal musicians started playing a soft melody. Everyone turned to face the double doors at the entrance to the great hall. They slowly opened, and a young girl and boy started the procession. They were Sir Rodney's children, Christopher and Sarah. Christopher, who was eight years old, was dressed in a royal blue outfit similar to the one the royal guards wore, only in miniature but without the feathered hat. He was carrying a white satin pillow to which two delicate gold rings were attached with a silver ribbon. Sarah, a sandy-haired six-year-old-girl was clad in a floor-length pale pink silk gown festooned with tiny red roses. In her left hand, she held a straw basket that was filled with delicate red rose petals. She would put her little hand into the basket, retrieve several rose petals, and toss them in front of her.

Behind the ring bearer and flower girl walked Princess Charlotte. She was breathtakingly beautiful in a pale pink silk gown, almost the duplicate of the gown the flower girl wore. Her golden tresses were pinned up, and she wore a small gold tiara on her head. Princess Charlotte was so exquisitely beautiful that Carl could not take his eyes off her as she slowly walked toward the center of the hall to the rhythm of the music playing softly for the wedding procession.

Princess Audrey slowly walked into view of the doors. She was being escorted down the aisle by Sir Paul who was clad in his new deep blue clothing as commander of the royal guards of Castle Alauria, complete with a white feather in his cap. Princess Audrey's gown was white satin with a layer of delicate hand embroidered white lace over the top of the satin. There were hundreds and hundreds of tiny white pearls sewn onto the embroidered lace. Her dark brown hair with red highlights shimmering throughout was worn down and over her shoulders flowing in soft curls. She wore a long veil and had a gold tiara adorned with rubies atop her head. There was a fifteen-foot white lace train attached to her shoulders, and it, too, had hundreds of tiny white pearls sewn all over it. Princess Audrey was absolutely stunning. Lord Lawrence was entranced by her beauty as she slowly walked in his direction. He was smiling broadly and kept saying over and over softly to himself, "*This lovely vision is my bride. I can't believe how lucky I am.*"

King Stephen conducted the wedding ceremony, and the guests were weeping tears of joy by the time it was over.

As is tradition in Alauria, when someone marries a royal personage, they automatically become royalty themselves. Therefore, Lord Lawrence henceforth shall be known as Prince Lawrence.

King Stephen, Prince Lawrence, and Princess Audrey led everyone to the dining hall where the royal chef and his staff had brought the wedding dinner and laid it out on the tables. There were venison roasts, fresh fish in cream sauces, roasted pork over which was spooned thick gravy, chicken simmering in wine, beef in light sauces, and all sorts of vegetables and fruits were on platters throughout the room. One silver goblet filled with wine, and one gold goblet filled with mead were placed by each guest's plate.

King Stephen stood and proclaimed, "Let us all raise our goblets to toast the bridal couple."

Everyone stood, lifted up their silver goblets.

Sir Paul said, "We all wish you a long, happy life together, and may you both be blessed with many healthy, happy children."

Prince Lawrence and Princess Audrey stood up and walked to the center of the dining hall where they proceeded to enjoy the first dance of the evening to the sweet sounds of the royal musicians. Others joined them, and soon the dance floor was almost immovable with so many people swaying to the music. Carl wanted to dance with Princess Charlotte, but he felt as a commoner he did not have the right to ask her. He was happy just to be able to steal glances at her all evening. She even caught him looking at her as she was stealing glances in his direction all evening too. They both smiled and quickly looked away at those moments when their eyes met.

The happy festivities continued until the wee hours of the morning.

CHAPTER 49

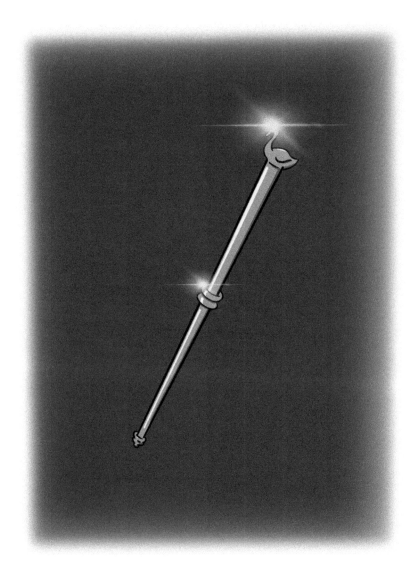

Carl spent the night in the castle, and in the morning, he changed back into his woodsman garb. Carl wanted to thank the king for treating him so graciously. He walked up the grand stairway to

King Stephen's royal bedchambers. When he approached the double doors, King Stephen's royal guards moved aside to let him knock on the door.

One of the royal guards inside the king's chambers opened the door and motioned for Carl to enter. "I am glad to see you this morning, Carl. There are some things I would like to discuss with you," said King Stephen kindly.

"It seems that a lot of things have changed in our kingdom since you arrived several weeks ago. Please be seated while I send for Sir Paul, Sir Rodney, Prince Lawrence, Princess Audrey, and Princess Charlotte. We all wish to talk to you about a few things."

Within minutes, everyone assembled in the king's chambers and seated themselves around his vast table. "Before we begin, I would like Princess Charlotte and Carl to fetch me my royal scepter from the library and don't return without it," commanded the king.

Carl and the princess looked at King Stephen with questioning looks, as he should have sent one of his royal guards on this simple errand. But, as he is the king, they acquiesced and left to fulfill his wishes. They walked down the royal staircase and down the hallway to the entrance of the library. Carl, not seeing anything that resembled what he believed a royal scepter looked like, asked the princess to describe it.

"Father's royal scepter is a long gold ornamental staff topped with a golden swan," the princess told Carl.

He asked the princess if she knew where it was and if she had found it yet.

"It isn't here," said the princess.

"We can't return until we find it," reminded Carl. So, they continued searching every nook and cranny. Finally they sat down on one of the benches, and Carl said, "What do we do now?"

"I don't know. It has always been either here by my father's favorite reading couch or up in his bedchambers," replied the princess.

"I guess we are stuck here and must continue to look," said Carl.

The princess looked at Carl and said, "I really need to thank you for rescuing me from the evil baron. We have not been alone together since we left Gladstone Castle, so I could not thank you properly. I am deeply grateful, Carl."

"I would do anything for you, Princess Charlotte," said Carl looking into her deep blue eyes.

Just as his heart fluttered whenever she called him "Carl," her heart fluttered whenever he called her "Charlotte."

The princess returned Carl's direct gaze, and the two of them sat there, not saying a word, comfortable just sitting there. They were looking at each other for several minutes when from above them, hanging over the gallery railing, they heard Prince Lawrence saying loudly, "Good grief, Carl. Take her hand and then kiss her!"

Instead of being embarrassed and standing up, Carl did as instructed. He took Princess Charlotte's right hand in his left hand, pulled her close to him, and kissed her. As she had been holding Carl's locket the entire time they were on the hunt for the king's scepter, the princess quickly put the locket into her pocket and took Carl's right hand in her left hand and kissed him back.

"I have wanted to kiss you since I first laid my eyes on you," said Carl.

"And I have wanted you to kiss me since I first laid my eyes on you," replied the princess softly.

They embraced and kissed again.

Prince Lawrence, now joined by Sir Paul and Sir Rodney, all leaned over the gallery railing again. "It's about time," said Sir Paul.

"Now that that is over, both of you hurry up and go directly to the king's chambers," said Sir Rodney.

"The king is waiting…for you both, not the royal scepter. He has that in his chambers," said Prince Lawrence as the men turned away from the gallery railing, chuckling.

CHAPTER 50

The wise king knew, and everyone else had known, that Princess Charlotte and Carl had fallen in love but didn't know it themselves. After their kiss and discovering that they really did love each other, they returned to the king's royal chambers. The future of Alauria was laid out before them in that wonderful meeting, everyone completely forgetting about the royal scepter.

The first thing King Stephen said was, "I would like to formally thank you Prince Lawrence, Sir Rodney, Sir Paul, and Carl on my behalf and that of the entire kingdom of Alauria for rescuing Princess Charlotte and bringing her back home safely." King Stephen was beaming with pride at these four heroes.

"We hoped to hold a special celebration feast in your honor," he continued, looking at each of the men in turn, "but with Princess Audrey's wedding and the other important changes, I shall elaborate on fully in a few minutes, we just don't have time right now. In one month's time, we shall all assemble in the great hall, along with the happy citizens of Alauria and hold that special celebration honoring each of you," he added.

"On behalf of the four of us, I would like to say that we were honored to be of service to you, Your Majesty, Princess Charlotte, and Alauria, sire," said Sir Rodney.

"In addition to Prince Lawrence, Sir Rodney, Sir Paul, and Carl, the celebration will also honor the wizard, Dreaddrick, Hans, Andrew, Frederick, and Lily for their parts in saving and protecting Princess Charlotte," said King Stephen.

The king touched on many important topics affecting each and every person seated at the table and some not present.

"The wizard, Dreaddrick, is to officially become the royal wizard for all of Alauria. He will be on call for both my castle and for Gladstone Castle. Dreaddrick will continue to live in his own home when he is not needed at either castle," said King Stephen.

"Andrew is to be the royal mason and continue to reside in Castle Gladstone," said Prince Lawrence. "When needed in Alauria, he will be sent for and will reside during his stay here with his uncle. Douglas is elated with Andrew's new position and that he will be able to spend time with him."

"And Hans has been elevated to royal stable master at Gladstone Castle," said Sir Rodney.

"Frederick has always been chef at Gladstone Castle, but he is to be the royal chef of Gladstone Castle now," said the king.

Sir Rodney said, "Frankie and Silver will each receive a Medal of Honor for their participation in aiding us in the Black Forest."

"Lily, in turning her home into a safe haven for Princess Charlotte, and aiding Carl in his endeavors, is to be given the title, 'Lady,'" said Sir Paul proudly.

"Princess Audrey and I are not going to live in Gladstone Castle after all. We are going to stay in Alauria and reside here in King Stephen's castle," said Prince Lawrence.

"Since Sir Rodney is to be commander of Gladstone Castle's royal guards, he and his family are going to move to Gladstone immediately after the festivities are over tomorrow evening," said King Stephen.

"My wife, Lady Rosemary, and our children, Sarah and Christopher, are very excited about this move. It is going to be a real adventure for them," said Sir Rodney.

"Sir Paul is going to remain in Alauria's castle as commander of the royal guards," said King Stephen. "But he is not going to live in the castle itself. He thinks that your cottage, Carl, is a perfect home to raise a family. Sir Paul had gotten to know Lily and her sons while he was in Gladstone Castle, and he is going to marry Lady Lily. Sir Paul will bring Lady Lily, Jake, and Billy here to live in your cottage, Carl. They are planning on adding two rooms in the back, not large rooms but just big enough for the boys to sleep in one while Sir Paul and Lady Lily can sleep in the other."

"Tommy had taken to Sir Paul as soon as he met him," said Carl happily. "Tommy can live with Sir Paul and Lady Lily. It will be exciting for him to have Jake and Billy to play with too. But I would like to come and visit Tommy and all my other woodland friends often."

"Of course," replied Sir Paul happily.

CHAPTER 51

Carl was more than happy to give his cottage to Sir Paul and Lady Lily. He would no longer be living there. Carl returned to his humble wooden home in the forest immediately after King Stephen's meeting was concluded. He had a lot to take care of before the next morning. He inspected every inch of the cottage and furniture to make sure that everything was perfect. He wanted Sir Paul, Lady Lily, Jake, and Billy to have the best home possible.

Carl had hand-carved every piece of furniture over the years. The round table and four chairs were the first ones he made. Sally and Arnold Chipmunk posed for the backs of the chairs. They happily chatted with Carl as he painstakingly etched their images carefully on the wood. Several times he had to chastise them to sit still. They loved to play and found it hard to stay in one position for more than four minutes at a time.

Jill, Bill Deer, and their son Ricky all posed for the legs supporting the big round table in the kitchen area. The three of them didn't mind standing without moving for long periods of time. They were fun to talk to while Carl carved their sleek legs and smiling faces.

Carl walked over to the bed headboard. Here Raymond Raccoon proudly sat posing on the kitchen table so Carl could stand up while carving the headboard. Raymond Raccoon got overly excited while relating the story of Betsy Badger falling into the stream while playing tag. Raymond was so animated that he fell off the kitchen table. Carl immediately jumped back to rush over to Raymond to make sure he was not hurt. In his hurry he had gouged the wood a little too much. Raymond Raccoon's image on the headboard now has three ears instead of two. Thankfully Raymond was not hurt physically. It just was his pride that was injured when he fell. Carl picked him up and petted him from his head to his back for several minutes while his little raccoon friend calmed down.

"Please don't tell anyone that I fell off the table, Carl. I would be very embarrassed if my friends found out," pleaded Raymond.

"Don't worry, Raymond. It will be our secret," soothed Carl.

The table that held his books was carved with Sammy Skunk's image. That was the hardest one for Carl to complete. Even though it was the smallest piece of furniture Carl carved, it took the longest in time. Sammy wasn't used to keeping his tail still for long periods of time without playing with his friends. While posing he would swish his tail periodically. The trouble was that when he swished his tail, he would forget he was indoors and that he shouldn't emit his special perfume.

"Hey, cut that out, Sammy," chided Carl on many occasions. Carl had to actually leave his cottage and go outside and catch a breath of fresh air while Sammy's fumes cleared out.

Finally the table was finished. The carving of Sammy was one of Carl's best pieces of work.

The best model Carl ever had was Chester, his elderly turtle friend. Chester didn't mind standing in one position for hours on end. Several times Carl walked over to Chester to see if he was still awake. Chester said, "If I fall asleep, you will know it. Peter Porcupine told me that I snore very loudly when I sleep."

After that, Carl didn't bother to check if Chester was awake or asleep. In fact, at least two times Carl heard Chester snore. Peter was right, Chester snored louder than anyone or any animal Carl had ever heard before.

None of the animals that posed for Carl minded being his models. They were proud that Carl would use their images on his carvings. They also enjoyed spending time talking with their special human friend.

Carl lovingly looked at his ornately-carved highboy where he stores all his dinnerware and food supplies. Here he had carved many of his feathered friends. He looked at images of Robby Robin, Chucky Cardinal, Milton Oriole, Jessie Sparrow, and Reginald Wren. The birds would pose for about ten minutes each. Then they would fly around his cottage and land back where they started. Carl never had to ask them to make the same pose. Each and every one of them resumed the same position when they returned. It was difficult getting their feathers exactly right, and it took Carl quite a while to learn how to chip out feathers in the wood, but once he learned how to do it, he relaxed and held some interesting conversations with them.

Carl learned that each of the birds like different foods. Some preferred berries while others didn't like berries at all. Every one of them enjoyed taking dips in the stream. They played in the water every day. Some of the birds built their nests up high in the trees, others preferred low bushes. He always knew they had different calls.

Carl had learned their various chirps and tweets when he was a young lad.

As Carl looked around his cottage, he fondly remembered how all his animal friends happily chattered away while he painstakingly duplicated their features on each piece of wood. He knew that Lady Lily, Sir Paul, Jake, and Billy would cherish each and every piece of furniture as he does.

Carl strode to his closet and pulled out his large leather bag. He gathered his few personal belongings and put them inside the bag. He walked to the door and turned back to take one last look at the cottage and its contents. Carl smiled at all the fond memories he gathered while living here. He was also smiling as he would have many more new and very happy memories now. The entire time Carl was walking through his cottage, Tommy was close by his side. He would rub up against Carl's legs every time Carl stopped to look at a piece of furniture.

While Carl was walking through the little forest in the direction of King Stephen's castle, he started to whistle some of the happy tunes he heard the royal musicians play when he first set foot inside the castle. Tommy kept pace with Carl every step of the way. He lifted his tail proudly and flicked it back and forth to signal to all the critters living in the woods. Carl's animal and feathered friends joined him and Tommy in their walk. Everyone was very excited.

Upon reaching the edge of the forest he turned to face all his friends, smiled and said, "I will return often and visit with you."

Each of the animals and birds wished him happiness and knew in their hearts that Carl would keep his word.

Carl turned and walked across the lush green velvet lawn. The swans glided smoothly on the silver lake leaving trails of soft ripples as they gracefully swam to the edge of the lake to acknowledge Carl's presence. He smiled down at them. Then he walked to the open drawbridge and walked across it, his feet hardly touching the thick wooden planks. He was almost floating on air.

Prince Lawrence greeted him as he reached the entrance to the castle. "Today is the most important day of your life, Carl."

"I know. Time is running out. I must prepare for the event now," said Carl as he handed his leather bag to Prince Lawrence's outstretched arm.

The two men hurried up the stairs. The door to Carl's new chambers was open. Inside Carl could see that his bath was already prepared. Fresh clothing was laid out on the large four-poster bed.

Two man servants aided Carl in removing his simple clothing. Carl happily stepped into the waiting tub filled with warm water and aromatic oils. While in the tub, one of the servants shaved Carl so perfectly his face never felt so smooth. Another servant trimmed his hair.

Three servants helped Carl out of the tub and into royal blue velvet pants, a white silk shirt, and a royal blue velvet jacket. There were no trimmings on this suit. None were needed as the clothing was perfect in itself. His boots were made of the finest leather Carl had ever felt.

Prince Lawrence was impatiently waiting in the hallway for Carl's pampering to be completed. He was pacing back and forth like a father awaiting the birth of his first son.

Carl opened the door. Prince Lawrence said, "Finally. Let's go."

The two men rushed through the hallway, down the stairs, and into the Great Hall where King Stephen stood in the center of the room upon the single rose and swan emblem of Alauria. Streamers of silver ribbons entwined with roses were strung throughout the room. Upon seeing Carl, the king smiled and motioned for Carl and Prince Lawrence to quickly join him.

Hundreds of people were standing on each side of the room leaving a six-foot wide path for Carl and Prince Lawrence to walk through. They approached the king and stood on his left.

Two minutes later the royal musicians began playing a soft melody. Two small boys in deep maroon velvet outfits slowly walked into the room. Jake was on the left with Billy on the right. They were smiling at Carl standing by the King. Each child bore in his hands a white satin pillow upon which a single ornate gold ring was tied with a silver ribbon. Jake carried the one with Carl's ring while Billy held Princess Charlotte's. Billy walked so purposely and deliberately that no one would have guessed until recently he could not move his legs. Keeping pace with the beat of the music, the young lads moved toward the center of the room. There they turned and stood on the king's right. Carl gave them both a wink and a smile.

Directly behind the ring bearers walked young Sarah. She wore a floor length pale mint green silk gown with tiny white roses embroidered all over it. The straw basket in her hand was overflowing with delicate white rose petals. Sarah smiled and tossed the petals in front of her. She then joined Jake and Billy by King Stephen's side.

Princess Audrey entered the room. She wore a pale mint green silk gown very similar to the one Sarah was wearing. Princess Audrey's dark brown hair shimmered with beautiful red highlights reflecting in the candlelight of the large room. Her coif had been gathered in intricate braids on top of her head. Tiny white roses were entwined in the braids. Her green eyes were sparkling and had never shown so beautifully before owing to the exquisitely colored gown she was wearing.

A hush fell over the room. The beautiful Princess Charlotte accompanied by Sir Rodney stood at the entrance of the great room. Sir Rodney wore the deep maroon military uniform as Commander of the Gladstone Castle royal guard, closely matching the suits worn by Jake and Billy. Princess Charlotte was a vision of beauty. Her white satin gown accented her perfect figure. Over the satin was a layer of fine, hand embroidered white lace. Tiny red roses were embroidered all over the lace from the tips of her delicate fingers, to the high neckline, to the flowing folds of the gown sweeping the floor. Her golden tresses were worn down cascading in soft curls to her shoulders. Atop her head she wore a gold tiara in which tiny rubies and pearls were embedded. Attached to this tiara and her shoulders was a fifteen-foot lace train. Sewn into the train were hundreds of tiny rubies. Sir Rodney's uniform perfectly accented the roses in the lace and the rubies in Princess Charlotte's tiara and train. Around her neck, a simple gold locket was the only jewelry worn by the bride. As breathtakingly beautiful as the wedding dress was, Princess Charlotte out-shown the fabulous garment. She was glowing.

As Princess Charlotte moved closer down the aisle towards Carl, he felt like her exquisite blue eyes were a deep, deep ocean. The nearer she glided towards him, the deeper he fell into the blue water of her eyes. Princess Charlotte's beaming smile and dancing eyes never left Carl's face as she moved closer to where he was awaiting his bride. Carl was completely captivated. He always knew she was beautiful, but the vision coming toward him was indescribably elegant and stunning. For the first time in his life Carl was speechless.

While King Stephen presided over the wedding ceremony, a few tears of complete happiness could be seen trickling out of the corner of Carl's eyes. Carl's beautiful princess of his dreams was no longer a dream. She was now his very own real princess.

The celebration was enjoyed by all. There was only one minor incident which occurred about an hour after the festivities had begun. Dreaddrick was summoned and abruptly left the party. A short while later a courier brought a message from the wizard. It read: *King Stephen, I would like to thank you for your gracious invitation to the marriage of Princess Charlotte and Carl. I extend my deep apologies for leaving their wonderful wedding reception so quickly. In my hurry not to be late for the ceremony I tied my dragon, Dudley, to the vegetable garden fence. I knew he would become hungry and he could graze in the garden to fulfill his appetite. It never occurred to me that he would also eat your entire hot pepper crop, his favorite treat. Dudley ate so fast that he got the hiccups. Don't worry; I replaced the burned fence around the garden. I had him fly us to the river so he could quench his thirst and get rid of his hiccups. The few treetops he burned along the way will fill in with fresh leaves in a short period of time. Respectfully yours, Dreaddrick.*

PS: I have sent 200 boiled fish to your kitchens. They will make a good dinner for your guests to partake of tomorrow evening. And as soon as the river water cools down I will restock it with brook trout and the various other fish that Dudley inadvertently cooked while curing his hiccups.

Tomorrow, immediately after the nuptial festivities are over, Princess Charlotte and Prince Carl will travel in the golden carriage to Gladstone Castle and live there,

HAPPILY EVER AFTER.

ABOUT THE AUTHOR

 Linda and her husband, Lee, have resided in Virginia for almost forty years. Her passion has always been writing both full-length novels and short stories. Lee was a Lieutenant Colonel in the United States Marine Corps. Linda stopped working outside of the home to raise their family of four rambunctious boys, Marc, Jason, Jim and Jon. In her spare time, she and her typewriter/computer spent many happy hours together. Their sons were Linda's inspirations for most of her stories.

Linda's interest in writing had followed her throughout her entire life beginning before elementary school when her mother presented her with an old manual Remington typewriter. She used this relic to produce her elementary school's newspaper. She graduated to electric typewriters while working as assistant press secretary for a political committee where she wrote speeches for senators and other politicians. Then with the introduction of computers, she became editor of four Cub Scout packs and Boy Scout troops newsletters. In her spare time, she was editor of *Hobby Greenhouse News* and assistant editor of *Hobby Greenhouse Magazine* as well as assistant editor of *The Latest Dirt* for the Master Gardener Association of Central Rappahannock Area.

Linda was also published with a feature article in *The American Gardener* for the American Horticultural Society. She ghostwrote a book *Simplified Self-Defense for Women* by William M. Charles II as well as worked on the *Windjammer,* the Aquia Harbour Community Magazine.

As you can tell, Linda and writing are one.

CPSIA information can be obtained
at www.ICGtesting.com
Printed in the USA
LVHW041459310720
662069LV00002B/87

9 781645 441618